LITTLE BLUE MARBLE 2019

2019

CLIMATE IN CRISIS

EDITED BY KATRINA ARCHER

A Ganache Media Book

Vancouver

If you are reading this book as a PDF, you have obtained a pirated, unauthorized edition, and are contributing to the marginalization of authors' incomes. We hope you enjoy your latte, which cost more than an authorized edition of this book, and took a fraction of the time to prepare.

If you bought this book, thank you, and we unironically hope you're enjoying it with the best latte you ever tasted. You probably tipped your barista too, because you're awesome.

This book is a work of fiction. Names, characters, places, and incidents either are the product of the authors' imagination, or are used fictitiously. Any resemblance to actual persons, living or dead, events, or locales is entirely coincidental.

LITTLE BLUE MARBLE
2019
CLIMATE IN CRISIS

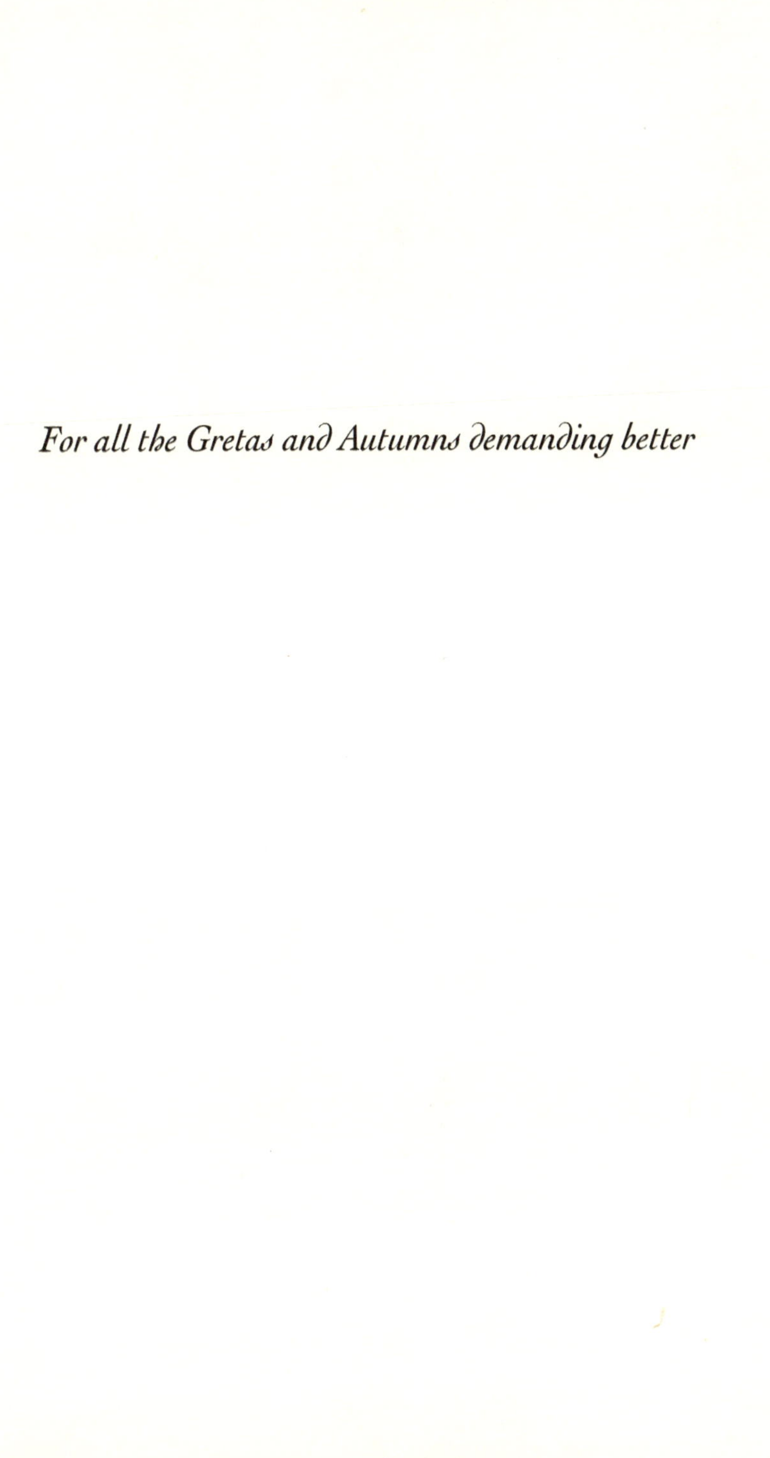

For all the Gretas and Autumns demanding better

CONTENTS

INTRODUCTION

Welcome to the collected stories and poems of *Little Blue Marble* from 2019. All of these stories are available for free online because *Little Blue Marble*'s mission is to educate and inspire, not to make a profit. We thank you, however, because your purchase of this anthology will help us bring you more great stories about the climate crisis, and keep our mission on track.

As I write this, Extinction Rebellion is leading road and bridge closures in cities around the world, in a concerted effort to get our political leaders to wake up and do something about the climate crisis. Greta Thunberg inspired millions of students and marchers around the globe in one of (if not the) largest global protests ever. Young indigenous water protectors like Autumn Peltier are on the front lines of environmental activism. The Green New Deal promises to be a major election issue in the USA. Children are suing governments to try to force action on climate.

And yet, governments worldwide still subsidize the fossil-fuel industry and invest in new infrastructure. Greenhouse gas emissions are up, with global carbon use rising instead of trending downwards like we need it to if we are to have any hope of mitigating disaster.

Little Blue Marble 2019 is our small contribution towards raising awareness. The momentum is building, and more voices are speaking out and demanding action. Change—the right sort of change—is still possible.

It has to be.

— *Katrina Archer, Publisher & Editor,* Little Blue Marble

RABBLE-ROUSING

Lorraine Schein

Call a strike against this world
for a bluer one, a purpler one;
one where arms will never fail
to embrace us against darkness.

Protest the deaths of friends and love.
Protest science without magic.

Picket for an Earth with imaginary colours
and more moons.
Picket for life in an alternate dimension,
where all can fly
and birds can speak.

This world force-feeds us logic and offices,
locks us out of childhood
and nights prone to stars.
Protest light pollution.

Demand free passage for us borderliners
and equal pay for thoughts.
Demand cats' rights
and floral equality for dandelions.

Boycott splinters and paper cuts.
Boycott Mondays.

Be a troublemaker, be demonstrative.
Hug a cloud! Organize lightning strikes!
Stand with the tigers' blockade.

Incite a slowdown against time flying.
Join a silent march for more snow and new glaciers.

Provoke a riot against tight underwear.
Stage a walkout from nightmares.

This is a direct call to indirect action,
an indirect call to direct action.

Resist gravity—
uprise skyward!

ABOUT THE AUTHOR

Lorraine Schein is a NY poet and writer with interests in anarchist ideas. Her work has appeared in *Strange Horizons*, VICE *Terraform, Syntax and Salt*, and *Star*Line* and in the anthologies *Gigantic Worlds, Tragedy Queens: Stories Inspired by Lana del Rey & Sylvia Plath*, and *Aphrodite Terra. The Futurist's Mistress*, her poetry book, is available from mayapplepress.com. "Rabble-Rousing" was partly inspired by the writing of the 19th-century American anarchist, Voltairine de Cleyre.

FROM *ADVANCED HUMAN BIOLOGY, 2ND EDITION*

Elizabeth Rubio

When the changes first manifested, humanity called it a disease.

The first change affected blood. While the pH of human blood at the time was usually maintained at roughly 7.4, many people began to show a long-term blood pH of higher than 7.6. These people, remarkably, did not suffer the symptoms commonly associated with alkalemia: muscle pain and spasms. Instead, these individuals enjoyed a normal life, although some data indicate that osteoporosis was more common in affected individuals in the first 100 years the condition was observed. This may have been merely a correlation rather than a result of the changes to blood pH. Importantly, blood from affected individuals was not compatible for transfusion to unaffected individuals, and vice versa. Indeed, if individuals with high-pH blood received transfusion from those without the condition, they often suffered acidemia, including muscle weakness and seizures. Research eventually revealed that individuals with high blood pH carried a novel mutation in the gene for V-ATPase, causing changes to the enzyme that led to an increase of carbonate ions in the blood. These people benefited from high levels of atmospheric carbon dioxide.

Shortly after this change appeared, a change in the composition of adipose tissue in many people emerged. Epigenetic changes were responsible for this shift, which saw a transformation of white adipose tissue to brown adipose tissue, along with a substantial increase in the amount of adipose tissue persisting throughout development and into adulthood, which was associated with a slow metabolism and low body temperature (average 34 degrees Celsius, or 93.2 degrees Fahrenheit). Although these people were first viewed as merely obese, as global temperatures entered what has become known as the Great Heat, these individuals were afforded many levels of protection. In the hot temperatures that became pervasive in the tropics and subtropics, the lower body temperature of those with high levels of brown fat meant that they suffered rarely, if at all, from heat exhaustion or heat stroke. They were additionally able to metabolize the fat in their tissues to generate water, allowing them to survive for as much as thirty days without access to water of any kind. In extreme cold, such as that associated with the localized harsh winters that became common after the Great Heat, these individuals entered a state of hibernation, not unlike that once seen in the now-extinct brown bear.

The final change (and at this point no one was still calling these changes disease) was neural, in both the supramarginal gyri and lateral frontal pole. Prior to this change, only the right supramarginal gyrus was associated with empathy. Today, both the right and the left gyri control this vital social response. Additionally, the lateral frontal pole grew substantially, giving modern humans their characteristic foreheads and allowing for the increase in long-term planning necessary for environmental disaster aversion and restoration. At the same time, the nucleus accumbens underwent a small degree of restructuring, although debate remains as to whether this change had any effect on reward-seeking and long-term planning behaviour. More research into this field is needed.

These changes, which occurred over a mere four generations, had significant biological and social consequences.

Phylogenists disagree regarding exactly when modern humans (*Homo consiliens*) split from our more primitive ancestors (*Homo sapiens*), but it is generally agreed to have happened sometime between 200 and 300 years ago. For a few generations, hybrids of *Homo consiliens* and *Homo sapiens* were common, and it was difficult to tell the difference between protohumans, *Homo sapiens*, and modern humans, *Homo consiliens*. Surprisingly, many protohumans were hostile toward humans and hybrids, possibly a result of their undeveloped left supramarginal gyrus. This led to a decrease in interbreeding, resulting in a genetic segregation of the two *Homo* populations. As the humans flourished, the ability to produce viable offspring with protohumans was lost.

Socially, the protohumans became more and more tribal, seeking to isolate themselves as much as possible. At first, this was allowed to proceed naturally, as these hominids became extremely hostile and often violent if humans approached them. Over time, however, it became clear that their numbers were dwindling, and the International Council agreed that intervention was necessary. The protohumans were moved to environments most suited to their biology and given as many resources as possible. They were encouraged to breed, and the hardiest offspring were moved among preserves in an effort to increase overall genetic vigour. However, the lack of effective physiological structures for surviving the high-carbon-dioxide atmosphere and temperature fluctuations eventually proved fatal to the species. The last surviving member died merely eighty-six years ago.

Today, a great deal of study is devoted to this species. After all, their history is our history, and they kept abundant written records dating back millennia. There is even some debate about naming them protohumans, as some scholars prefer simply "human." Their loss is a tragic event, one of uncountable millions of species that perished as a result of the Great Heat.

ABOUT THE AUTHOR

Elizabeth Rubio lives in Austin, Texas, where she writes science fiction and fantasy, as well as nonfiction. Once a professional biochemist, she believes very strongly that every person is a scientist. She hopes the optimistic scientists of all kinds can work together to create a future for us all. When not writing, she can be found snuggling her cats or at the library. Find her other stories in *Analog* or *Mythic*, or look for her nonfiction series from Enslow Publishing.

UNDER THIS ROCK

Andrew Dana Hudson

Jacob crouched in the cattails, working on his patience. It was hot as hell, even as the sun went down. Jacob wanted to wet his dry lips on the water, but he knew that wasn't safe. Instead he watched the rainbow slick of oil slide towards him, tugged by the subtle suction of the thirsty reeds. Before he was mayor, he'd designed this wetland to use the heat and dryness the Harpies had brought to better clean the water. But that chemical swirl, runnelling down from the hills, made all that work moot. In five days some kid in Rock Springs would be pouring that poison out of the tap. Jacob shifted half an inch, kept patient. The seed carbine was heavy on his back.

Sitting there, Jacob thought about the Harpies. He'd lived through a few—everyone had. Once you'd been battered by a superstorm, seen your land shrivel with drought, the sober diagnosis "climate change" didn't cut it. The winds were monstrous now, wrathful, mythic things. The fossil poison the frackers were digging up there had brought down the Harpies. Jacob would see it put back in the ground.

So when the sliver moon was up and the floodlights in the hills snapped on, Jacob climbed out of the reeds and up the hill. Beside him the others did the same. At the edge of the drilling site, they paused to listen to the company men within, who shouted to be heard over the clatter of their ancient generator.

"Decadents." Julianne spat in the dirt next to him. "Shoulda kicked 'em out just for that guzzler, mayor."

Jacob shushed her, instead motioning up at the lights. Julianne and her brothers shouldered their rifles, and Jacob ticked down his fingers. A crack, and the lights sparked out. Jacob prayed that'd be the only bulletgrass they would plant tonight.

They moved then, and had the frackers under gun before they could shine up their phones. Six carbines against thirty guys. Bad ratio for everybody.

"Evening, fellas." Jacob strode two steps forward, symbolically in the crossfire. "We're here to serve you some paperwork."

"The fuck you are—" the foreman said. Even with the yards between them, Jacob could tell the foreman was a hand taller than he was. "Wait, you're that mayor, huh? Motherfucker who pulled the plug at Jim Bridger." The big man showed teeth. "I heard about you."

"That's right." Jacob tapped his city crest pin out

of habit. "Got a duty to protect my people, and that coal-fire spewer was what was hurting them most."

"Your citizens really gonna see it that way when a calm, cloudy day knocks out their HVAC and TVs? I know them Bridger techs. They spent good money in your town, just like us. You think your citizens are gonna get to missing that after a while?"

"I guess we'll find out," Jacob said, gritting his teeth. "But for now, I'm on to the next one. It is my sorry duty to remind you that the city of Rock Springs has rescinded your lease on this place. I'm going to request that you shut your pumps down and pack up."

The foreman rocked on his heels, relaxed. Jacob decided the men weren't about to charge them just yet. He nodded to Julianne, and she headed towards the humming pump tower that loomed behind them. She kept her knees bent the whole time, like a hunting cat, taking her eyes off the frackers only when she reached the pump controls. The foreman's gaze followed her.

"You know, I did get that notice you sent," the foreman said. "I think you've got your bureaucratic wires crossed tonight, Your Honour. That eviction's been suspended, pending review by *the state*. Or didn't you hear from our lawyers?"

"State and I are having a bit of a disagreement these days." Jacob could smell the unnatural stink of the tailing ponds. "And since they're preoccupied while Denver holds Cheyenne, I'm afraid this will have to be a forgiveness-not-permission type situation."

"Come on, mayor, we're good business. We support your schools, gave a big contribution to the policeman's ball." The foreman grinned again. "I notice it ain't police you got with you tonight. So what are you doing this for? Bunch of whiny fugees out west pay you off?"

Jacob let the slur roll around the site for a moment, then called out. "Julianne! You can turn that nonsense off."

"Now just hold it!" the foreman flared. "This is a delicate operation. Lotta work went into setting those pumps right. I won't be responsible for what happens if some amateur shuts it down improper."

"Then maybe you can give us a hand doing it right," Jacob said. "Because it's going off tonight, one way or the other. Go on. Your men can stay put. You go help Julianne over there. She won't bite."

"Mayor," Julianne called out. "I looked at the imaging they got. Caprock looks okay, but they been pumping a while."

The foreman didn't move. Instead he kept bargaining.

"Water troubles? We'll cop to that. Generous settlement. You got good dinos down there, friend, and the right people still pay well for that. Plenty of profit to go around."

"Afraid this is about the rock," Jacob said. He

fingered the carbine's safety. "It's got uses long past the flash of gas you're digging up. Californians say that under this rock they can shove away some of the carbon that's brought the Harpies. Thing is, this rock isn't any good if you break it first. And the Californians, they outbid you."

That last wasn't true, but Jacob knew it was something the company men would understand, even if they didn't like it. They muttered amongst themselves.

"That's not good," the foreman growled. "'Cause my dinos, they're already on the books. Bosses borrowed off them to pay our wage, and I'm not about to turn those numbers red for the sake of your fucking Cali-fugee-loving bullshit!"

Then there was a change in the air. Jacob saw frackers' fists clench, hands move to belts. A couple of them had to be packing, he knew. If Julianne's brothers lost control of them, they might not get another chance at the rig.

"Julianne!" Jacob called again. "Hit it off!"

She did, and there was a clatter, and a strange silence descended upon the site. The frackers growled, agitated by the loss of that filthy hum.

"You fuckers!" the foreman snarled. "Who are you to interfere in our business? You don't work for us, you don't invest. You're barely even a customer. What right do you or Rock Springs or anyone have to tell us what to do with land we paid for?"

"I breathe the air." Jacob knew it wouldn't help, but he wanted to make the case anyway. "I drink the water. And I live under this wicked sky, just like you, and the Californians, and everyone else on this planet. I say we get a say."

He felt a tremble then, some primordial quiver before the violence. Jacob knew blood was about to spill. Could see it all in his mind's eye. They'd get charged, and there'd be shots, but the seed ammo in their guns wasn't always lethal. There'd be a tussle, and they would lose, and heaven help his people back home when these frackers called their company. The tremble became a shake.

And the frackers did charge, but as they did, the earth heaved. Jacob's feet left the ground. He felt his gun fire into the sky as the wind left his chest.

By the time he got a breath, the frackquake was already over—and so was the scuffle. The frackers had been mid-run when the ground shook out from under their legs. They lay in a tangle, while Julianne and her brothers held steady crouches. Of their circle, only Jacob was on his back.

His mind ran to his town, thinking of the damage, and to the huge rock under them, which might have just cracked. His fault—he'd given the order—but only a little bit. Still gasping, Jacob walked to the prone foreman and kicked him hard in the jaw.

"Another Harpy your books have brought on my people," Jacob spat. "Only just this once, she came for you."

They ziptied the frackers and bullied them into the container trucks their rig had come in. Julianne sent the trucks back the way they came. California's drones would be there by morning to check the rock.

"That coulda gone bad, mayor," Julianne said as they headed towards town. "All luck. We gotta get better."

"Yeah, we will," Jacob said. "First time for everything. But we're a power now, so there'll be more. Lot of rocks in Wyoming the world will need."

Past his wetland they walked. Cattails rustled in the night wind. Beneath the water they tugged, made tiny flows, a biological tide. Jacob was done being patient, waiting for the tide of history to change. He'd grow his own tide from now on.

ABOUT THE AUTHOR

Andrew Dana Hudson is an award-winning speculative fiction writer. He studies sustainability at Arizona State University and is a fellow and researcher at the ASU Center for Science and the Imagination. He is associate editor at Holum Press, which publishes *Oasis*, a Phoenix-based journal of anticapitalist thought. His work envisions the lived experiences just around the corner in our post-normal world, and the struggle to make good choices in the climate crisis.

THE SOFT EYES OPEN

Bo Balder

The first hint of change was my son's eye colour.
At breakfast one morning a shaft of sunlight struck
Kai's eyes. They were golden brown, with irises that
seemed to swallow the whites. For a moment I was
sure they'd been grey before, the next second I berated
myself for being the kind of dad who doesn't even
know his kid's eye colour. Better that than the other
option that loomed large and threatening.

I didn't say anything but focused on getting him to
finish his cereal and out the door in time. He'd just
turned thirteen, not yet in the full throes of puberty,
no longer a child either. But he actually liked school,
so my job wasn't too hard most mornings. It was just
that Madison had always done breakfast, and I think
the daily reminder flattened our morning moods.

When he biked off I grabbed our only physical
album from the shelf, to look for the kiddy pool
snapshot I knew was in there. He looked up at us—
Madison was still alive then—from his rubber ducky

with this tranquil expression, his eyes definitely grey against the caramel glow of his face.

I immediately thought of the Chimera, the threat I'd been in denial about since I first noticed his eyes. The Chimera only struck children, whose bodies were still plastic enough to survive the change into a different species. Many people think the Chimera is nature's way of replacing what it has lost. All the large land and sea animals are extinct. Gone are the elephant, the blue whale, the hippopotamus, the buffalo (again), along with thousands of other, less picturesque species. The Earth's ecology is a complex machine. Even now we don't know what made it work before we destroyed it.

But there were no tests to detect the Chimera early. I went to work simmering with anxiety, afraid that if I voiced my fears I would make them come true.

I didn't discuss it with Kai. I should have, but my tongue floundered every time I thought of bringing it up. He'd been having a hard time with Madison's death, not surprisingly, and I wanted him to be happy and carefree for a bit.

My days blew by in a haze of fear. I noticed every child with odd tufts of hair or discoloured nails. I worked harder than I ever had just so I could get home in time to eat dinner with Kai.

One morning Kai only grunted when I asked how

he'd slept.

I winced at the look of surprise and hurt on his face, still sweet and round with those all-gold eyes, no whites anywhere.

"Kai?" I said. "What's up?"

I knew with absolute certainty what he wanted to say: "Dad, I can't talk! My tongue doesn't work!"

His face turned purple with effort. He grabbed my forearm with his hot, sticky hands and grunt-shouted at me.

He looked six instead of thirteen, overwhelmed by this sudden powerlessness.

"Kai," I said. Why hadn't I spoken before? Because I thought he was too young. Because I wanted to protect him from the uncertainty. And now I had hardly any time left. His understanding of the spoken word would leave him as surely as his grey eyes.

"I think it's the Chimera."

He shook his head violently. He must have thought of it himself. He was a smart kid and his school had been stricken by cases as much as any school on the planet, about 1% of the children so far. "I'm so sorry," I said.

He was silent. Tears dripped down his face. I opened my arms and he burrowed into them like a toddler. There was no cure. We didn't even know which virus or activated junk gene caused it, although the blogosphere was rife with speculation. Speculation was all we had, because science takes time. The disease needs years to fully develop. It has to change every cell in his body.

My heart broke when he stepped out of the embrace with a look at the clock and got his backpack. As if getting to school on time was important now. He'd never finish school. When his transformation was done, he'd be sent to whatever place on Earth his new species inhabited.

When he came home from school, covered in dirt, scrapes, and bruises, because kids are merciless, I set him down at dinner. "I'm going to quit my job," I said. "You don't have to go to school anymore. We can do fun things together as long as possible."

Kai shook his head again, in that new, violent way. He grabbed a pad and started writing. I felt like such an idiot for not thinking of that. His fine throat and tongue motor control was gone, but not his writing. Yet. "I want to stay in school," he wrote. "I want to be normal."

My face buckled and cracked. What a terrible idea. Wasn't today's experience enough to know that normal no longer applied to him? He couldn't possibly want to go through that every day.

I didn't need to say what I thought. He frowned as he deduced my reaction. He was such a smart kid. That was going to go, too.

"What did the other Chimera kids in school do?" I

asked, playing for time. My answer was going to be vital to our relationship.

He shrugged and waggled his left hand first, then his right hand. Some stayed, I translated, some stayed away. I looked at him for a long time. I couldn't treat him as a child any more. Most thirteen-year-old animals are adults.

I took a deep breath and said the hardest words ever. "Kai, I have no control over what school and the Chimera Disease Center are going to say. But until that time, it's your choice. I will support whatever you want."

His face crumpled and he ran out of the room, too old and too proud to let me see his tears.

Later that day, the school contacted me to tell me they had alerted the CDC. They arrived that same evening, suited up and all, to take Kai away. I didn't appreciate the circus they put me and Kai through, but I knew better than to protest. There have been cases of Chimera where the parents lost custody trying to keep their kid out of the maelstrom.

The long and short of it: the diagnosis was confirmed. *Huang vs. School District of Columbia* had ruled in favour of Huang a couple of years ago, so Kai still retained his right to education.

Kai went back to school, but already he was getting clumsy on his bike, his hands thickening into we didn't know what kind of paw or hoof or claw. His writing became nearly illegible, until one day he gave up on it. He ate voraciously of everything except meat, growing at a vast rate in all directions. Clearly he wasn't going to be anything small or delicate. Or carnivorous.

A bump swelled between his eyebrows. The skin felt rough. We pored over animal atlases and picture books. Some librarian had pasted red stickers over the large extinct mammals, which was pretty much all of them by now. Giraffe, lion, orca.

What if he turned into a walrus? Or a bottlenose dolphin? How would I ever keep track of him?

Kai threw the books away and went digging for his old picture books. I wondered about his temper. But he returned with a shoddy children's book, the kind you get for free, with garishly coloured cartoon animals. He pointed at the unicorn, from its golden spiraling horn to his own tiny bump.

My heart sank. I picked up the fallen books and found the rhinoceros.

Kai refused to look at it, working his lower jaw from side to side in a peculiar grimace. In his coarsened, yellowing teeth and budding tusks I saw proof of my suspicion.

I read out loud to him. "The rhinoceros is a herbivore. It's thought to be the second-biggest land mammal in the world. The rhino averages about 1.5 tons in weight and has a tough skin that is roughly ¾-

inch thick. It has a large horn in the middle of its face and some species have a second smaller horn above the larger one.”

Kai crept back on my lap, although by now he weighed almost twice as much as me, and pointed at the words with his clumped hand, the fingers merging with the palm. “Unh! Unh!”

I pushed away premature plans of how to transport him to Africa and started over. “The rhinoceros is a herbivore …”

My voice burred on, thick and clogged. Maybe I could become a ranger at Kruger National Park.

ABOUT THE AUTHOR

Bo lives and works close to Amsterdam. Bo is the first Dutch author to have been published in *F&SF* and *Clarkesworld*. Her fiction has also appeared in *Escape Pod*, *Nature*, and other places. Her SF novel *The Wan* was published by Pink Narcissus Press.

For more about her work, you can visit her website (www.boukjebalder.nl) or find Bo on Facebook.

THE WAY OF WATER

Nina Munteanu

She imagines its coolness gliding down her throat. Wet with a lingering aftertaste of fish and mud. She imagines its deep voice resonating through her in primal notes; echoes from when the dinosaurs quenched their throats in the Triassic swamps.

Water is a shape shifter.

It changes yet stays the same, shifting its face with the climate. It wanders the earth like a gypsy, stealing from where it is needed and giving whimsically where it isn't wanted.

Dizzy and shivering in the blistering heat, Hilda shuffles forward with the snaking line of people in the dusty square in front of University College where her mother used to teach. The sun beats down, crawling on her skin like an insect. She's been standing for an hour in the queue for the public water tap. Her belly aches in deep waves, curling her body forward.

There is only one person ahead of her now, an old woman holding an old plastic container. The woman deftly slides her wCard into the pay slot. It swallows her card and the light above it turns green. The card spits out of the slot. The metre indicates what remains of the woman's quota. The woman bends stiffly over the tap and turns the handle. Water trickles reluctantly into her cracked plastic container. It looks like they have another shortage coming, Hilda thinks, watching the old woman turn the tap off and pull out her card then shuffle away.

The man behind Hilda pushes her forward. She stumbles toward the tap and glances at the wCard in her blue-grey hand. Her skin resembles a dry riverbed. Heart throbbing in her throat, Hilda fumbles with the card and finally gets it into the reader. The reader takes it. The light screams red. Her knees almost give out. She dreaded this day.

She stares at the iTap. The dryness in the back of her throat rises to meet her tongue, now thick and swollen. She gags on the thirst of three days. Just like her mother's secret cistern, her card has run dry; no credits, no water. The faucet swims in front of her. The sun, high in the pale sky, glints on the faucet's burnished steel and splinters into a million spotlights …

• • •

Hilda read in her mother's forbidden book that water was the only natural substance on Earth that could exist in all three physical states. She'd never seen enough water to test the truth of that claim. She remembered snow as a child. How the flakes fluttered down and landed on her coat like jewels. No two snowflakes were alike, she'd heard once. But not from her mother; her mother refused to talk about water. Whenever Hilda asked her a question about it, she scowled and responded with bitter and sarcastic words. Her mother once worked as a limnologist for CanadaCorp in their watershed department, but they forced her to retire early. Hilda tried to imagine a substance that could exist as a solid, liquid, and gas, all in the same place and same time. One moment flowing with an urgent wetness that transformed all it touched. Another moment firm and upright. And yet another, yielding into vapour at the breath of warmth. Water was fluid and soft, yet it wore away hard rock and carved flowing landscapes with its patience.

Water was magic. Most things on the planet shrank and became more dense as they got colder. Water, her textbook said, did the opposite, which was why ice floated and why lakes didn't completely freeze from top to bottom.

Water was paradox. Aggressive yet yielding. Life-giving yet dangerous. Floods. Droughts. Mudslides. Tsunamis. Water cut recursive patterns of creative destruction through the landscape, an ouroboros remembering.

She'd heard a myth—from Hanna, of course—that

Canada once held the third richest reserve of freshwater in the world. Canada used to have clean sparkling lakes deep enough for people to drown in. That was before the unseasonal storms and floods. Before the rivers dried up and scarred the landscape in a network of snaking corpses. Before Lake Ontario became a giant tailings pond. Before CanadaCorp shut off Niagara Falls then came into everyone's home and cemented their taps shut for not paying the water tax.

When that happened, her mother secretly set up rainwater catchers on her property. Collecting rainwater was illegal because the rain belonged to CanadaCorp. When Raytheon and the WMA diverted the rain to the USA, her cistern dried up and they had to resort to getting their water from the rationed public water taps that cost the equivalent of $20 a glass in water credits. It didn't matter if you were rich —no one got more than two litres a day.

Hilda and her mother hadn't seen a good rain in over a decade. Lake Ontario turned into a mud puddle, like Erie before it. The Saint Laurence River, channelized long ago, now flowed south to the USA, like everything else.

One day the water patrol of the RCMP stormed the house. They seized her mother's books—except Wetzel's *Limnology*, hidden under Hilda's mattress—and they dragged her mother away. The RCMP weren't actually gruff with her and she didn't struggle. She quietly watched them ransack the place then turned a weary gaze to Hilda. "We were too nice … too nice …" she'd said in a strangled voice. She didn't clutch Hilda to her bosom or tell her that she loved her. Just the words, "We invited them in and let them take it all. We gave it all away …" It took a long time for Hilda to realize that she'd meant Canada and its water.

CanadaCorp wasn't even a Canadian company. According to Hanna, it was part of Vivanti, a multinational conglomerate of European and Chinese companies. When it came to water—which was everything—the Chinese owned the USA. When China finally called them on their trillion dollar debt, the bankrupted country defaulted. That was when the world changed. China offered the USA a deal: give us your water, all of it, and we'll forfeit the capital owed. And they could stay a country. That turned out to include Canadian water, since Canada had already let Michigan tap into the Great Lakes. That's how CanadaCorp, which had nothing to do with Canada, came to own the Great Lakes and eventually all of Canada's surface and ground water. And how Canada sank from a resource-rich nation into a poor indentured state. Hilda didn't cry when her mother left. Hilda thought her mother was coming back. She didn't.

• • •

A tiny water drop hangs, trembling, from the iTap faucet mouth, as if considering which way to go: give in to gravity and drop onto the dusty ground or defy it and cling to the inside of the tap. Hilda lunges forward and touches the faucet mouth with her card to capture the drop. Then she laps up the single drop with her tongue. She thinks of Hanna and her throat tightens.

The man behind her grunts. He barrels forward and violently shoves her aside. Hilda stumbles away from the long queue in a daze. The brute gruffly pulls out her useless card and tosses it to her. She misses it and the card flutters like a dead leaf to the ground at her feet. The man shoves his own card into the pay slot. Hilda watches the water gurgle into his plastic container. He is sloppy and some of the water splashes out of his container, raining on the ground. Hilda stares as the water bounces off the parched pavement before finally pooling. The ache in her throat burns like sandpaper and she wavers on her feet.

The lineup tightens, as if the people fear she might cut back in.

She stares at the water pooling on the ground, glistening into a million stars in the sunlight.

• • •

Hanna claimed that there was a fourth state of water: a liquid crystal that possessed magical properties of healing. You could find it in places like collagen and cell membranes where biological signals and information travelled instantly. Like quantum entanglement. The crystalline water increased its energy in a vortex and light. Hanna seemed to know all about the research done at the University of Washington. According to her, this negatively-charged crystallized water held energy like a battery and pushed away pollutants. She told of an experiment in Austria where water in a beaker, when jolted with electromagnetic energy, leapt up the beaker wall, groping to meet its likeness in the adjoining beaker. The beaker waters formed a "water bridge," like two shocked children clutching hands.

Hilda's mother had dismissed Hanna's claims as fairytale. But when Hilda challenged her mother, she couldn't explain why water stored so much energy or absorbed and released more heat than most substances. Or a host of other things water could do that resembled magic.

Something Hilda never dared share with her mother was Hanna's startling claim about water's intelligent purpose. She cited bizarre studies conducted by Russian scientists and some quasi-scientific studies in Germany and Austria suggesting that water had a consciousness. "What if everything that water does has an innate purpose, related to what we are doing to it?" Hanna had once challenged. "They've proven that water remembers everything done to it and everywhere it's been. What if it's self-organized, like a giant amoebic computer? We've done terrible things to water, Hilda," she said, sorrow vivid in her liquid eyes. "What if water doesn't like being owned or ransomed? What if it doesn't like being channelized into a harsh pipe system or into a smart cloud to go where it normally doesn't want to go? What if those hurricanes and tornadoes and floods are water's way of saying 'I've had enough'?"

None of that matters now, Hilda thinks rather abstractly and feels herself falling. They are all going to die soon anyway. Neither water's magical properties nor Hanna's fantasies about its consciousness are going to help her or Hanna, who disappeared again last month.

• • •

"I can't do this anymore with you," Hilda ranted. She paced her decrepit one-room apartment and watched Hanna askance. Hanna sat on Hilda's worn couch like a brooding selkie. Like a sociopath contemplating her next move. Waiting for Hilda's. "This is the last time." Hilda kept her voice harsh. She wanted to jar Hanna into crying, or something, to induce some kind of emotional breakdown. In truth, Hilda was so relieved to see her itinerant friend, alive and well, after her lengthy silence. Hilda went on, "It's always the same pattern. After months of nothing, you come, desperate for help … water credits or some dire task that only I can perform … then you disappear again, only emerging months later with your next disaster. I never hear from you otherwise. I don't know if you're dead or alive, like I'm a well you dip into. Like that's all I mean to you. Where do you go when you disappear? Where?"

She dropped back in the lumpy chair across from Hanna and watched her gypsy friend, hoping for some sign of remorse, or acknowledgement, at least. She knew Hanna wouldn't answer, as though every question she asked her—particularly the personal ones—was only rhetorical in nature. Hanna just stared at her like a puppy dog. As if she didn't quite understand the problem. She could barely speak at the best of times. Hilda had decided long ago that Hanna was partly autistic. Maybe a savant even; she was inordinately clever. Too clever sometimes. Maybe she'd been traumatized when she was little, Hilda considered. Apparently, the emergence of sociopathic behaviour was created—or prevented—by childhood experience. She knew that Hanna's childhood, though privileged with significant wealth, was terribly lonely and troubled. Her parents, who both worked in the water industry in Maine, spent no time with her and her sister. Like obsessed missionaries, they were always travelling and tending their water business. When Hanna was in her late teens, her parents perished in a freak accident.

Hanna had avoided any cross-examination, but

Hilda's uncompromising research on Oracle uncovered a strange story—a common one in the old water wars. Hanna never revealed her last name but Hilda guessed it was Lauterwasser, the name of a known water baron family in Maine: John and Beulah Lauterwasser owned a large water holding of spring water near Fryeburg and sold *Apa Fina* all over the world. They'd refused buyout offers by the international conglomerate Vivanti. Soon after the Lauterwassers drowned, the holdings mysteriously came into the hands of Vivanti. Hilda suspected foul play. Not long after that, Hanna appeared in her life.

From the moment Hilda saw her, seven years ago, she'd felt a strange yet familiar attraction she couldn't explain. A bond that commanded her with a kind of divine instruction, a *déja vu*, that bubbled up like an evolutionary yin-yang mantra: *you two were born to do something important together*. Hilda felt a strange repelling attraction to her strange friend. Like the covalent bond of a complex molecule.

Like two quantum-entangled atoms fuelled by a passion for information, they shared secrets on Oracle. They corresponded for months on Oracle; strange attractors, circling each other closer and closer— sharing energy—yet never touching. Then Hanna suggested they actually meet. They met in the lobby of a shabby downtown Toronto hotel. Hilda barely knew what she looked like but when Hanna entered the lobby through the front doors, Hilda knew every bit of her. Hanna swept in like a stray summer rainstorm, beaming with the self-conscious optimism of someone who recognized a twin sister. She reminded Hilda of her first boyfriend, clutching flowers in one hand and chocolate in the other. When their eyes met, Hilda knew. For an instant, she knew all of Hanna. For an instant, she'd glimpsed eternity. What she didn't know then was that it was love.

Love flowed like water, gliding into backwaters and lagoons with ease, filling every swale and mire. Connecting, looking for home. Easing from crystal to liquid to vapour then back, water recognized its hydrophilic likeness, and its complement. Before the inevitable decoherence, remnants of the entanglement lingered like a quantum vapour, infusing everything. Hilda always knew where and when to find Hanna on Oracle, as though water inhabited the machine and told her. Water even whispered to her when her wandering friend was about to return from the dark abyss and land unannounced on her doorstep.

Hilda leaned back in her chair with a heavy sigh. She always gave in to Hanna. And Hanna knew it. "OK," Hilda said. "What do you need this time?"

Hanna's face lit with the fire of inspiration and she leaned forward. "Oracle told me something."

Hilda slumped deeper in her chair and rolled her eyes. "Of course Oracle told you something. It always does."

Some cybergenius created Oracle after the Internet sold out to Vivanti. The Oracle universe was the last commons, Hilda considered. It had brought her and Hanna together, bound them into one being with a common understanding. Hilda discovered one of Hanna's sites. It turned out to be a code for what was happening to water. To Hanna's obvious delight, Hilda decoded her blog and like two conspiring teenagers, they shared intimate secrets about water. Hilda shared from her textbook and Hanna embellished with facts that Hilda's mother reluctantly confirmed or vehemently denied. Hilda never discovered how Hanna got her information, how she managed to cross the Canadian/US border or who Hanna really was. Whether she was a delusional charlatan, the itinerant daughter of a murdered water baron, a water spy for the US, or something worse. Hilda realized that she didn't want to know.

"I was right but I was wrong too," Hanna said, beaming like an angel. "Mandelbrot has the last piece of the puzzle. It's right there, in Ritz's migrating birds and Scholes' photosynthesis." She lifted her eyes to the heavens then grinned like an urchin at Hilda. "… In Schrödinger's water." Seeing Hanna this way, lit with genuine inspiration, Hilda knew she would totally give in to whatever plan the girl had concocted. She wasn't prepared for what Hanna asked for.

"I need a thousand water credits."

"What?" Hilda gasped. "You know I don't have that! What the chaos do you need it for?" Hanna had inherited a hoard of water credits in the Vivanti settlement but had lost them all, through various wild ventures and a profligate lifestyle. Over the years, Hilda, who had barely anything, had given Hanna so many water credits for her wild schemes during their strange friendship. She'd funded Hanna's Tesla-field amplifier, her orgonite cloud-buster and anti-HAARP electromagnetic pulse device. Hilda had never once gotten any proof of them having amounted to anything, except to keep Hanna hydrated.

Hanna inched forward in her seat and her eyes glinted like sapphires. "You know about the nanobots that keep the smart clouds in the States from coming north over the border?"

Hilda nodded, wondering what Mandelbrot's fractals—and photosynthesis—had to do with weather control and cloud farming. It was part of the deal the US made with the Chinese, who had first perfected weather manipulation with smart dust. Vivanti owned the weather. Canada, which had been mined dry of its water, was just another casualty of the corporate profit machine.

"Why do you think water lets them do that?" Hanna said.

Hilda squirmed in her seat. What was Hanna

driving at? As though water had any say in the matter.

Hanna wriggled in her seat with a self-pleased smile. "What if those nanobots 'decided' to let the clouds migrate north?"

Suddenly intrigued, Hilda leaned forward and stared at her friend. "Are you talking sabotage?" she finally said in a hoarse whisper and wondered who Hanna really was. "How?"

Hanna grinned in silence. A kind of conspiratorial withholding look. She always did that, Hilda thought: looked reluctant to say, when that was precisely why she'd come. To spill a secret. The two women stared at one another for an eternity of a moment. Hilda struggled to stay patient, understanding the hierarchy of flow.

Hanna finally confided, "Not sabotage. More like collaboration." She leaned back and her mischievous grin turned utterly sublime. She looked like a self-satisfied griffin. "Like recognizes like, Hilda. Have you ever noticed how children going for walks with their mothers notice only other children? The most successful persuasion doesn't come from your boss, but by a trusted colleague ... *a friend.*"

Hilda shook her head, still not understanding.

Hanna leaned forward and gently took Hilda's hand in hers. She pressed Hilda's fingers with hers in a warm clasp. Smooth hydrated fingers that were long and beautiful, not like Hilda's selkie hands. "It's ok, my friend," Hanna said. "Just trust me. Trust me one more time."

• • •

The faucet swims into a million faucets. Hilda understands that she is hallucinating. People generally stay away from the public iTap when someone in her condition approaches. People don't want to share, but they also don't want to feel cruel or greedy about not sharing. In today's blistering heat, urgency overrules decorum and they simply ignore her away. They know she is close to the end. She's seen others and has shied away herself. She feels the water guardians hovering. Waiting. If she doesn't get up and walk away, they will come and take her—probably to the same place her mother was taken. Someplace you never came back from.

It is a month since she gave Hanna everything she had in the world. A month since Hanna disappeared with Hilda's thousand water credits—worth a million dollars on the black market. Credits she borrowed off her rent. In that month, Hilda's entire world collapsed. Her research contract—and associated meagre income—ended suddenly at the Wilkinson Alternative Energy Centre, with no sign of transfer or renewal. Three weeks later, the Co-op wiped most of her bank account clean then locked her out. She found a piece of shade from the relentless sun under an old corrugated sheet of metal in the local dump, and set up camp there.

Nothing has changed with the water. No clouds have come. No rains have come. And no Hanna has come.

This time, Hilda knows that Hanna is really gone. That whatever fractal scheme Hanna had conjured, she's failed. Since they flowed into one another, they always seemed to know when the other was in trouble … Strangely, Hilda feels nothing. No presence, no absence. Just nothing.

Hanna is probably dead. Or worse. Since meeting her, Hilda has learned to monitor Oracle for signs of her elusive friend. Small blips of signature code on certain sites. Anonymous tags. Like ghosts, they wisped into existence, whispered their truths, then disappeared like vapour in the wind. Even they stopped. Hanna too has turned to vapour.

Hilda is alone. Doomed by her trust, her faith and her gift … All gone with Hanna …

No. Not all gone.

• • •

For every giver there must be a receiver in the recursive motion of fractals. Everything is connected through water, from infinitely small to infinitely large. Like recognizes like. Atom with atom. Like her and Hanna. Like water with water.

She's fallen recumbent on the dusty ground. She is dying of thirst metres from a water source. And no one is coming to help her. They just keep filling their containers and shuffling away in haste. She doesn't hate them for it. They aren't capable of helping her. She squints at the massive sun that seems to wink at her and chokes on her own tongue. Perhaps her vision is already failing, because a shadow passes before the sun and it grows suddenly dark. It doesn't matter.

She's given all of herself faithfully in love and in hope. Through Hanna. To water. She is two-thirds water, after all. Just like the planet. Water and the universe are taking her back into its fold. She will enter the Higgs Field, stream through spacetime, touch infinite light. Then, energized, return—perhaps as water even—to Earth or somewhere else in the cosmos.

Her mother was wrong in her angry heart. They weren't too nice. It is simply the way of water. They are all water. And water is an altruist.

It starts to rain.

Huge drops spatter her face, streaming down, soaking her hair, her clothes, her entire body. It hurts at first, like missiles assaulting her with suddenness. Like love. Then it begins to soothe as her parched body remembers, grateful.

Dark storm clouds scud across the heavens like warriors chasing a thief. She's vaguely aware of the commotion of people as they scatter, arms and containers pointed up toward the heavens. She smiles then feels her body convulse with tears.

Is that you, Hanna? Have you come to take me home?

ABOUT THE AUTHOR

Nina Munteanu is a Canadian ecologist / limnologist and author of award-nominated speculative novels, short stories, and nonfiction. She is co-editor of Europa SF and currently teaches writing courses at George Brown College and the University of Toronto. Her latest book is *Water Is…*, a scientific study and personal journey as limnologist, mother, teacher, and environmentalist. *Water Is…* was recently picked by Margaret Atwood in the NY Times as 2016 "The Year in Reading." www.NinaMunteanu.ca; www.NinaMunteanu.me

THE CITY WE BUILT IN LIFE

Thomas Broderick

Experience Arizona's Man-Made Treasures!

Julie's face was taken over by a big grin as she unfolded the map. Navigator for the day, the eight-year-old had the honour of sitting up front. Mom and Adam sat in the back. Still early morning, the family had just checked out of their hotel in Flagstaff. "Dad was so right," Julie yelled back to her mom. "Seeing the Grand Canyon yesterday was so much better than just pictures!"

"I'm glad you liked it, honey."

Returning her attention to the map, Julie put her finger on Flagstaff and traced the day's route. Just south of Winslow were the Seven Wonders of the Ancient World. Holbrook had the Monuments of Washington, D.C. Just east of St. Johns was their final destination: the Silent City.

"Come on Dad!" Julie called out through a crack in the window. "We gotta get going!"

Mom looked up from the family's guidebook.

"Close the window, Julie. The batteries take a little longer to charge in the winter."

Dad took the driver's seat five minutes later, a broad smile on his face to match his daughter's. "Okay, Navigator Julie, which way?"

"East on the freeway!"

The late January morning was bright and cold, and the side of the freeway was marked with piles of dirty slush. Within minutes the family exited the Flagstaff suburbs. All around them was pristine desert.

"It's gorgeous out here." Mom took a picture with her phone. "Nothing like East L.A."

"Kids, you should be happy we could get you out of school." Dad sipped his chicory. "Not everybody had a granddad who helped build the Silent City."

"My friend Vic does," Adam said. He was twelve. "Vic's granddad's ninety-five, but he still remembers. Came to my class last year to tell us all about it."

"It's just too bad they don't do the overnight field trips anymore." Dad frowned, but just a little. "When I was your age every class made the trip. It was like a pilgrimage."

"What's a pilgrimage?" Julie looked up from the map.

"It's an important trip to a special place," Mom explained. "Like the trip we're taking this week. The Grand Canyon is a really special place. So is the Silent City."

"Ah, okay."

An hour later the family arrived at the Seven Wonders of the Ancient World. From the central parking lot, each Wonder was a quarter-mile in a different direction. Adam got his way—they had to see the pyramid first.

"The Great Pyramid of Giza was the first of the Seven Wonders constructed in the mid-2050s." Mom read from the guidebook as the family made the short walk in their heavy coats. "Built from 2.3 million blocks of synthetic carbonized basalt, it represents what the pyramid looked like in pristine condition."

"Syn ..." Julie struggled with the word.

"Synthetic ... carbonized ... basalt." Dad said the words very slowly. "It's the same special rock the Silent City's made of. You see, there were so many blocks left over that they let artists choose what to build next. The Seven Wonders and all the other special places on your map are made from those blocks."

"Like LEGOs?"

"Just like LEGOs."

Adam rubbed the pyramid's smooth surface. "Too bad it's not like the one in Egypt. I really wanted to climb it."

"I don't think they'd let you do that." Mom pointed to two uniformed park employees standing near the path.

The family spent the rest of the morning exploring

the Seven Wonders. After much prodding from his mother, Adam agreed to take a picture with Julie. Squeezing together on Nebuchadnezzar II's throne in the Hanging Gardens of Babylon, the siblings gave Mom toothy grins for the camera.

The family ate lunch at a diner in Holbrook. Dessert was a rare treat: a piece of real chocolate cake.

"You spoil them, you know?" Mom cut up the thin slice into four equal portions.

"Might as well." Dad passed out the plates. "We never got to eat this stuff when we were their age."

Julie carefully lifted the bite of cake to her mouth. Closing her eyes, she let it melt on her tongue.

The taste was love and hope and happiness.

After lunch, the family continued to the Monuments of Washington, D.C. Julie spent the entire drive mastering how to pronounce "synthetic carbonized basalt."

"Dad, make her stop saying it!" Adam jumped out of the car the moment it stopped in the parking lot.

"Leave your poor brother alone." Dad took Julie in a big hug and spun her around. She squealed in delight. "Race around the Washington Monument?"

A little later they stood inside the Lincoln Memorial. Julie put her small hand on Lincoln's foot. "Is the real Mr. Lincoln still there, Daddy?"

"Well, yeah, but the water's about up to there." Dad pointed to Lincoln's chest. "You'd need a boat to go see him." Julie frowned. "It's okay, honey. Just the other day there was something interesting on the news. The man said that by the time you're my age, people will be able to walk to Mr. Lincoln again!"

"Maybe her great-great-grandchildren will," Mom whispered to Dad before raising her voice. "Adam, get off Lincoln's lap! I don't want us to get kicked out of here!"

It was late afternoon when the family set off for the Silent City. Dad exited the freeway, and the road became two narrow lanes.

"Nobody lives out here." Julie tapped on the window with her fingertips.

Dad took a deep breath. "That's why it was perfect for the Silent City. I don't think Grandpa ever thought that people would want to come see it, though." He smiled to himself.

Still twenty minutes away, the Silent City started to grow out of the horizon. Julie immediately perked up in her seat. At first, it was like looking at Los Angeles from the hills: rows of buildings extending for miles. Yet all of these buildings were the color of heavy rainclouds, all the same shape but different heights. The shortest was about ten stories. The tallest was about fifty. There were no windows or lights. Everything was stone. Everything was lifeless.

At the entrance, Dad showed his ID to the park ranger. "We have a reservation up at the hotel."

The park ranger taped a shiny sticker to the inside of the car window. "Enjoy your stay, sir." He even waved at Julie as the family drove off.

Julie pressed her face against the window. "It's like *A Christmas Carol,*" she whispered.

"What's that?" Mom asked. Every year on Christmas Eve she read aloud the old tale.

"It's like the city in the story. Dark and scary. You think Marley and all the other bad ghosts live here?"

"Let's see." Mom flipped the guidebook to the chapter on the Silent City. "The buildings in the Silent City were constructed from 350 million blocks of synthetic carbonized basalt. An additional 900 million blocks make up the seventy-foot-thick foundation." She read to herself for a few seconds before closing the guidebook. "No ghosts, honey. No bad ones, anyway."

Dad followed the signs to the hotel, and they arrived in the parking lot just before sunset. "Bundle up, kids. At night it's even colder here than in the desert."

The hotel took up the first floor of one of the dark grey buildings. There were no windows or signs, just a modest door that led into the lobby. Their room for the night was spartan but comfortable. The food at the hotel restaurant was simple but filling.

"Early to bed tonight, you guys," Dad said as they got up from the dinner table. "Tomorrow we're getting up before dawn to see the first block."

Adam groaned. "Why so early?"

"Sunrise is the best time to see it."

The next morning Julie was ready to go the moment Dad got out of bed. Adam took a bit longer, hiding under the covers until Julie tore them off. Mom took forever, as she insisted on dressing her children in every piece of winter clothing she had packed.

"Out to see the first block?" The hotel manager had a knowing smile on his wrinkled face as the family entered the lobby.

Dad checked Adam's parka one last time. "Yeah, first time for the kids."

"It should be all yours this morning. Tomorrow night a hundred folks from Phoenix will be up here. One of those new religions. I think they're going to pray to it."

Dad and the hotel manager chuckled.

Outside it was freezing and blustery, yet the morning twilight promised dawn and warmth. Dad led the way. "It's not too far. Just one building away."

The walk took five minutes. At the end of it was a large clearing, a break in the Silent City's endless pattern. In the center was the first block.

The block was a perfect cube a foot taller than Dad. It didn't look any different from the innumerable others that made up the Silent City, the Monuments of Washington, D.C., and the Seven Wonders of the

Ancient World.

"Why is it here all by itself?" Julie patted it. "It's lonely."

Dad took Julie's arm. "Over here, honey."

On one side of the block was an engraved message. It read:

This is the first block of synthetic carbonized basalt to trap one ton of atmospheric carbon.

Produced in six hours at Sandia National Laboratories September 22nd, 2025

WE BUILT THE SILENT CITY SO NO MORE CITIES WOULD FALL SILENT

Mom rubbed the back of Julie's head. "You see, Julie, when Grandpa was your age, it was a scary time. People had put a lot of bad stuff in the sky. They couldn't see it, but it was hurting everyone. Then someone figured out how to suck it all out, just like our vacuum cleaner at home. The Silent City is all that bad stuff, but it can't hurt us anymore."

"But the real Mr. Lincoln," Julie stammered, furrowing her brow. "Then why ..."

Dad knelt to face Julie. "It was too late for Mr. Lincoln. It was too late for ..." He paused, and briefly looked at the ground before meeting his daughter's gaze. "It was too late for a lot of people."

"How many people?"

Dad put his hands on Julie's shoulders. "Remember yesterday when Mommy was talking about how many blocks are in the Silent City? All those big numbers? Now that we're here, can you imagine all those blocks, all the ones around us, all the ones we're standing on?"

Julie looked around. Morning's first light shone through the Silent City's thousands of nameless boulevards, streets, and alleys. Below her feet, level stone stretched on for eight miles in every direction.

Julie looked back at Dad and nodded slowly.

"That's how many people."

For a few minutes, the only sound in the Silent City was Julie's crying. Adam didn't tease his sister. He had cried, too, when he first learned about the Silent City in school. So had Julie's parents when they visited the Silent City as children.

Dad wiped Julie's face with a tissue. "Come on. Let's go." The family briefly embraced before walking back to the hotel, where warmth and breakfast awaited them.

There would be time later to visit the museum underneath the Silent City, learn about the sins of the past and the price humanity paid. Yet, more importantly, there would be the gentle reassurances that despite everything, life was still precious, and worth defending.

ABOUT THE AUTHOR

Thomas Broderick is a freelance writer living in the San Francisco Bay Area. His work has appeared in *Nature Futures*, *Persistent Visions*, and *Shoreline of Infinity*. He is a proud member of the Science Fiction & Fantasy Writers of America. He hopes to one day attend the Clarion Workshop. You can read more of Thomas's stories on his website: broderickwriter.com.

IN THE TEETH OF THE GALE

Ramez Yoakeim

I pressed the last hydrocorn shoot into its eyelet and secured the completed tray to the floating platform. Standing up, I swelled with pride looking at the swaying corn, and its canopy of oversized leaves. I marvelled at the ingenuity that turned the fragile corn of old into a crop that not only survived in the salty ocean, it thrived.

Squinting against the glare reflected off the water, I stretched my back, grown stiff from hunching over the trays. At twelve, I'm tall for my age, Mama says. Yet when the corn dances in the breeze, it looks like thirty-foot skyscrapers on the verge of toppling over my head.

"Agwambo, hurry. Baba's almost here!" My sister Baraka was five, nimble as a seagull, and twice as fearless. She roamed barefoot on the interconnected platforms that formed our farmstead, jumping over the gaps and ducking under pipes and machinery, like some pint-sized giggling ninja. I ran after her through the corn.

Mama and Bibi were waiting by the narrow tongue stabbing into the vast ocean, connecting the dock to the farm's platform. Bibi hung onto Mama's arm for support. She was born during the Troubles. As billions perished, she found a way to survive, riding the rising waters. The price was the hunch of her back, brittle bones, and milky eyes. Despite it all, nothing could bar her from her son's every homecoming.

The speck of the seaplane grew as it drew nearer, its solar-powered turbines wheezing in the breeze. Its belly bulged, like a giant pelican swooping down on a subsurface feast. Baba was gone on his routes for days at a time, moving goods between far-flung floating homesteads and the giant factory barges that crisscrossed between them. Even as far away as dry land.

Mama says there was a time when most people lived on land, before the oceans swelled and merged. No one could afford land now. Except for rich white folks, dry on their mountain tops.

I don't know why anyone would want to live on land, away from the breezes, infinite horizon, and yes, even the hurricanes. The only thing I envied about the land dwellers were the animals they kept.

Baraka slipped from Mama's hand and ran towards the moored plane. She reached it as Baba unloaded supplies, and a mysterious bundle. He flung a sack over one shoulder, and scooped Baraka up into the nook of his free arm.

"Baba got us a puppy!" Baraka's piercing shriek made my eyes water.

Mama's eyes lingered on my stunned disbelief for a moment, before she glowered at Baba. "I asked for a sewing machine to clothe your children. Instead you brought me a dog?"

"It's for Agwambo," Baba said. He winked at me and planted a kiss on her cheek. He handed me the puppy and leaned in low for Bibi to pat his head.

"What about me?" Baraka squirmed free and ran towards the puppy. It was black and white, with brown and beige spots, and tiny. Its paws were soft, its nose wet, and its tongue unexpectedly dry when it licked me. It was the oddest thing I had ever seen, and it was beautiful.

"Dogs eat meat, what do you propose we feed it, Baraka?" Mama teased. Her chagrin was as short-lived as clear skies. Baraka squealed with delighted horror, as she tugged on my shirt. I sat on my haunches and let her pet the puppy. He licked her face enthusiastically in return.

"Dogs eat whatever you give them." Bibi shuffled back towards the homestead. "They're survivors, like us."

"It'll be plenty happy with table scraps," Baba reassured her, before turning to me. "You'll need to come up with a name for it."

In Bibi's tales, names weren't given, they were revealed. Her stories spoke of heroes and kings of old, but I didn't see a reason why it should be any different for a puppy. I knew it would let me know what its true name was, in time.

• • •

When the hurricane claxon sounded, I was in the basement, hauling a sack of corn meal up to the kitchen for Mama. The watertight compartment under the farmhouse provided floatation support, dry storage, and—when one of the hurricanes that roamed the ocean got close enough to be a bother—shelter.

I dropped the sack and ran up the steps to a rapidly darkening sky. Roiling charcoal clouds raced towards us. Lightning lit the horizon with a curtain of purple-blue bolts.

Mama was helping Bibi towards the basement. My grandmother was not one to take reminders of her infirmity with grace. She yanked her arm free of Mama's hold. "I told you I'm fine, now leave me be."

"How will Baba land in this weather?" I asked.

"He'll probably wait it out somewhere safe," Mama reassured me, but the worry etched on her face told me she didn't believe it herself.

"Your father knows what he's doing," Bibi chimed in. "Worry about your little sister. I haven't seen her since breakfast."

That's what Baraka did: roam.

Mama called her name a few times, but even without howling winds, the farmstead was too large for Mama's voice to reach its every corner.

"I'll find her." I ran off before Mama could object. Despite her protests, Bibi needed help getting down the steep steps to the basement, and I'd rather Mama did that than me.

Running barefoot on the wet, foam-like, interconnected panels that formed the farm's platform was nothing new to me, but with wind gusts as forceful as whale blow, and just as unpredictable, I kept slipping, struggling to keep my footing.

"Baraka," I bellowed at the top of my lungs. Perhaps she was lost among the corn. I refused to entertain the possibility she'd gone overboard, into the choppy, roiling water.

I alternated between calling her name, parting corn clusters in the hope of finding her cowering safely between the stalks, and peering into the churning, frothy water, wondering if I'd be able to tell if she floated by.

Then I heard the puppy. It had managed a bark or two before, but now all it could do was whimper. Consumed with finding Baraka, I hadn't thought of the puppy at all. Shame descended upon me thicker than the rain now hammering the platform. I was not yet used to having a puppy. *It's only been two weeks*, I told myself.

Suddenly, the platform heaved, rising metres in the air, before crashing down into a void as the wave passed, sinking as deeply as it had risen. I hit the foam face first, but had no time to collect myself before a torrent washed over me, carrying me towards the water.

I scrambled for purchase, grasping at anything within reach. I blinked salt water from my eyes, sliding, the platform's edge rushing towards me, when another lurch of the platform sent me careening backwards towards the corn, having come within arm's reach of the edge.

I grabbed the corn stalks, wedging myself between them, as the pitching and flooding continued. With reason returning, panic set in. If I had come that close to being swept away, what chance did a little girl and a puppy stand of avoiding that same fate?

"Baraka," I screamed over the howling storm and thunder. "Baraka!"

In response, I only heard whimpering. I pressed towards it. Sound in a storm plays tricks on you. It's as if the air itself bends and curls, and with it the sound. At first it sounded like it came from the left, then from the right, then behind. I called until I was hoarse. Straining and listening for the whimpers, I saw my quarry.

The puppy had its jaw locked on Baraka's arm. I

don't remember how I closed the distance between us, swinging from one clump of stalks to the next, like chimps swung between branches in the vanished Earth of old.

The puppy had wedged itself inside a cluster of stalks, sitting on its haunches. Through a narrow gap in the thicket, it clenched the sleeve of a limp Baraka. No wonder whimpers were all I heard. It was all it could do with its mouth closed.

As soon as I reached Baraka, the puppy let go and began barking. I checked her pulse. She was alive. A dark gash marred her forehead, but the rain kept washing away the blood as it oozed from the wound.

I threw her over my shoulder, holding onto the corn with the other hand. The puppy's barks took on a frenetic tempo, an urgency borne of desperation, when it realized I was going to leave it behind.

With only two arms, I could pick between holding onto Baraka, hauling the puppy under an arm, and hanging onto the corn, but not all three.

Even as the storm gathered force, and its electric tentacles grew nearer, I stood frozen in place, struggling with a logistical problem for which there were no solutions.

"I'm sorry little one." I stared at the pup's large black eyes. "I'm not sure whether you should try and follow, or stay put between the stalks until the storm is past. I know I don't have any right to ask this of you, but please forgive me. I can't leave my only sister behind, and I risk us all if I try to take you too."

With tears mixing with the salty spray and sweat on my face, I spared the puppy of my dreams one last glance, and set off, determined not to look behind. It didn't follow. Its voice cut through the explosive tumult of the storm, neither barking nor whimpering now, but moaning. Long, desolate, soulful howls over which my guilt overlaid disappointment, and accusations of neglect and abandonment.

A minute or two later—for it's impossible to tell time in the middle of a hurricane—a deeper darkness fell over me. Instead of terror, I felt only exhaustion. It's as if we're capable of only so much emotion at one time, and when those reserves run dry, so does our capacity to feel anything at all.

"Agwambo, is that you?" It was Baba. Tall and strong Baba. Safe and protective Baba.

"Baraka is unconscious, and I had to leave the puppy behind, and he's scared, and—"

"Is it far?" Baba interrupted my ravings, even as he took Baraka off my shoulder and into his arms.

His question demanded no answer. I ran back, scooped up the puppy, and followed Baba's receding form. When I reached him, I grabbed the end of his shirt, like I used to when I was younger, much younger.

• • •

Huddled with the others in the basement, I complained, loudly. What good were hurricane warnings when they sounded just as the hurricane itself came bearing down on you?

Bibi huffed. "Children shouldn't be burdened by the cares of their elders. The day comes soon enough when they inherit them."

"That's the attitude that got us into this mess, Mama," Baba said in hushed tones. Baraka rested on his lap, in dry clothes with her wound dressed. "Let them think as they wish, and lead where they may. Who knows, it might be to our salvation."

Bibi sucked her lips, and turned towards the door, listening keenly to the raging storm.

"I know what its name is," I announced. Sensing my attention, the puppy raised its head and licked me. "Finding it out there renewed my hope, when it had been nearly spent. Everyone, meet Tumaini."

ABOUT THE AUTHOR

Ramez's academic research once involved engineering perfectly believable details out of nothing. Fiction seemed like the obvious next step. At one time or another an engineer, educator, and serial entrepreneur, these days Ramez devotes himself to charting humanity's future, one tale at a time. Find out more about Ramez and his work at yoakeim.com.

DILEMMA, WITH OMNIVORE

Keyan Bowes

Trust me, you do not want to go shopping with my mother. Mom has this passion for curiosities. Every shopping expedition is weird, whether in Dallas or Dar es Salaam or Delhi—like this time. (My mom's a diplomat, so we get around.)

• • •

On a hot Saturday afternoon in New Delhi, we're walking along the lane of stalls kept by Tibetan refugees, and Mom's checking every single one. In a tiny shop under a faded striped awning, she spots a baseball-sized round metal box with a grotesque face and four clawed legs. Something rattles inside, but the box won't open.

"What's this?" Mom asks. The guy just smiles and shrugs.

Mom's hooked. Something she can't identify? Curious. Something the shopkeeper himself can't identify? Even better!

She pays him Rs4,000 and doesn't even bargain. I

wave off the plastic bag he offers, and just carry the box in my hand. It's still closed, still rattling.

• • •

Soon after we get home, the globe splits along its equator, revealing a small porcelain egg.

Mom grimaces. "Mass-produced. Probably imported from China." She's disappointed that it's not handcrafted.

"Give it to me, then." I take it in my hand. The porcelain glows like really intense mother-of-pearl.

Mom likes the box, though, and puts it with her Delhi collection—old bronzes, inlaid marble paperweights, wooden elephants, and other assorted objects. The display cabinet's lighting makes everything look special whether it is or not. I leave my porcelain egg in there too, and go off to tussle with an assignment due tomorrow.

• • •

The next morning, the egg's in jagged pieces. The bronzes are gone and so is the side of the cabinet. From behind the couch peers a little scaly green animal with four bug eyes and two tails. It glances at me and emerges cautiously, looking hungry.

"Let's keep it, Mom!" I say when she comes in.

"Kris, it's eating the vintage bakelite lamp I found in Camden Market."

I quickly pile wood shavings from a carpentry project around the creature. It munches them like potato chips. I feed it a broken plastic bucket, and an old plastic brush from the kitchen. It polishes them off even faster. Then it sticks out a tiny purple tongue and licks its lips.

"It's so cute! Mom, we've got to keep it."

"No, Kris," Mom says firmly. "How would we cage it? It'll eat us out of house and home."

But what's she going to do with it? No animal shelter will take it, and we can't give it to friends. We don't even know where it came from—maybe Mars, home of little green men and the bug-eyed monsters? I decide to call him Bradbury, and tell only my closest friend Maya next door. We're both hoping to get accepted to the same college.

By Monday afternoon, Bradbury has eaten a pile of old clothes, a plastic curtain rod longer than himself (including his tails), vegetable peels from dinner, and the accumulation of polyethylene bags from grocery shopping. He's got no interest in any living thing, so the geckoes haunting the wall lamps are safe.

Then he escapes out the back door. I chase him, but he hides behind the marigolds in the garden. Now what? I really daren't let him get loose!

There's a sound of scratching. Bradbury abruptly emerges from the patch of orange flowers and I grab him. I know he won't bite me, but when I bring him back inside, he bites the dining table leg. I hastily give him my world history text. He delicately rips out each page and nibbles it appreciatively. Who knew a book could be so delicious?

"He's just like a puppy, Mom," I say soothingly. "Like your dog ate your shoe when you were a kid?"

"Kris, there's a difference between a puppy chewing on a shoe and a monster destroying a cabinet, a lamp, your textbook that we'll have to replace, and the dining table!"

Bradbury stays, thriving on whatever we feed him. He's particularly fond of anything plastic, which I suspect he's breaking down. All those hydrocarbons, essentially. The marigolds grow gorgeous and enormous from his manure.

• • •

When he's not eating, Bradbury follows me around. We don't play "Fetch!" any more because he eats the ball.

"Bradbury," I call one day, and he sort of squeaks at me.

"*Squeak squeaksqueak!*" I respond, and he copies me like a four-eyed two-tailed puppy squeaking up and down the scales.

Soon we're squeaking "Greensleeves" together. When Maya drops in, she teaches him some old Hindi film songs, and he learns to squeak "Dum Maro Dum" and a bunch of other tunes.

• • •

One evening, I hear Mom scream. I dash into the living room, to find Bradbury snacking on Mom's prized Kashmiri rug. I grab him, but it's too late.

"He has to go, Kris." Mom looks at the ruined carpet. "I'll talk to someone at the embassy. They'll find an agency to take him away." She stalks off to the kitchen to calm down.

I'm too horrified to say anything. They'll kill Bradbury, dissect him. I must stop this, but how? I huddle in my room, Bradbury curled up against me. His little purple tongue licks my cheek.

Maya comes over to commiserate. We tearfully feed Bradbury some waste plastic and an old polyester shirt.

Suddenly, I have an idea.

"Maya, didn't your Dad's company get the contract when the Indian government privatized garbage collection?"

"Yes?" Maya says.

"They have a big landfill outside the city, right? Bradbury could be their mascot?"

"Wow!" says Maya. "I'll ask Papa right now."

She goes outside to make the call.

"Papa wants to know, what'll happen when he eats faster than Delhi can produce garbage?" asks Maya when she returns.

"He'd need to be big as a T-Rex," I say confidently.

"Yeah." She looks at Bradbury. He's about the size

of a German Shepherd dog now.

"Maybe you can have a global garbage dump? All the countries will send their trash to your dad's company?"

Maya looks thoughtful, considering the logistics, then nods. "Papa should look for a landfill space near a port."

She calls him again.

• • •

"He's an ecological miracle," I tell Maya. "Maybe he'll solve our whole waste-stream problem."

"Right," says Maya thoughtfully. "But for how long? There has to be a limit to growth." She pulls out her tablet and starts some calculations.

"How long?" I ask her when she looks up.

"It's really a rough estimate now, but assuming he grows as big as an elephant, maybe five years?"

"Why an elephant? I know it's the largest land animal now but why not consider some of the extinct ones, if there's no food constraint?"

"Hmm. Those were larger … some may have been three or four times bigger than an elephant."

She plugs a few more figures into her calculations. "Anyway, he'll probably eat less as his growth tapers off. And that waste stream just keeps growing. Ten years?"

Maya's really into waste management. She's expecting to take over her family company one day.

"Wasn't I reading something about scientists breeding bacteria that can break down plastics?" I ask.

"Yeah," she says. "We have a company lab with a team working on it, and we hope to have something within ten years. But it's never going to be enough. In the end, if we don't shrink our waste production, we're still going to be buried in our garbage."

"So? At least it'll buy us time. Every bit helps. Recycling, composting … and Bradbury."

• • •

Three days later, we see Bradbury on TV, renamed Kachra-Nash (which means Destroyer of Trash) and happily munching through all the stuff Delhi throws away. Everyone assumes he's a CGI, except for Maya, her dad, and the landfill workers. And he's producing loads of excellent manure.

ABOUT THE AUTHOR

Keyan Bowes is a peripatetic writer of science fiction and fantasy based in San Francisco. She's lived in nine cities in seven countries, visited more (and is still travelling). These places sometimes form the settings for her stories. Her work can be found online in various webzines (including a Polish one), a podcast, and an award-winning short film, and on paper in a dozen print anthologies.

She's a graduate of the 2007 Clarion Workshop for science

fiction and fantasy writers, and a member of the Science Fiction and Fantasy Writers of America (SFWA). Keyan's website is at www.keyanbowes.org.

ARKUSHANANGARUSHASHUTU

Micah Hyatt

One hundred and thirty-one light years away from her body, Susan watched neon-yellow waves rush up a beach of blue sand to wash over her golem's bare feet.

It was a dead planet, without a trace of even microscopic life. Worthless except as the perfect vantage point from which to watch the first real-world test of Father's project.

A sun named Arkushanangarushashutu burned overhead. Father said that the word meant "the southeast star in the crab" in Babylonian. Susan loved saying it. It rolled off her tongue like a magic spell. Other golems stood on the beach, controlled by investors, shareholders, and researchers, all looking to the red-orange sky. A film of grey crept over the sun like a thin cloud as swarms of robotic ships laced themselves into a net around it. At Father's command, they would begin the resonance cascade that would kill the sun and capture its death throes.

"Arkushanangarushashutu," she said. No one

would ever stand here and say its name again. This was hello and goodbye. She crouched down and scooped up some blue sand, letting it sift through her golem's grey fingers. It clumped so nicely, she decided she would build a sandcastle.

She stuck her hands into the blue sand and scooped out the base of the castle. It was an activity that should have been mindless. But the part of her mind that came from her father considered the thing on a microscopic level—understanding that the wet sand clung together because water formed tiny bridges between sand particles and held them together with surface tension. She should decide how high she would like to build it before setting to work on the base to prevent running into trouble later. A little math was all it would take. A finger gouging notations into the beach.

A little ways down the beach, Father and Mother were walking together. Mother didn't want to be here. She hated having her mind in a golem, and she thought Father's project was a travesty. They'd been arguing about it for months, ad nauseam. Even now, minutes from the test, they were still arguing. They were too far away for Susan to hear them over the surf, but she could recite both sides of the argument by heart.

The Murder Dyson, Mother called it, trying to be pithy, oblivious that using the same mocking name for it every time was anything but. She'd say there was no reason for such an invention except grotesque greed. Father would respond with figures about mankind's exponentially growing power consumption. Tell her that the planets and the moons and even the asteroids at the fringes of this solar system had been scouted, so that nothing would be killed, not even on the molecular level. And Mother would lift her chin and accuse him of killing the constellations, killing beauty, rewriting the night sky for a smattering of joules. She might quote some horrible thing by Blake or Lord Byron. The poets would weep, she'd say. And he'd be quiet for a little while, because Blake and Byron cannot be argued with directly where beauty is concerned, but he'd break his silence with some awesome technical fact. Transmission of a supernova's worth of power across a gulf eight hundred trillion miles wide, delivered instantly to wherever needed through a side channel of the ansible network.

"Arkushanangarushashutu," Susan said, trying to block her parents' voices from her head. She had no argument of her own, no opinion on it. Their opinions clamoured so loudly she could not think on her own. But soon she'd be leaving them both, taking an elevator to an expensive orbital college paid for with Father's company money, and she did not know what she would study except that it would not be poetry or science.

The castle walls were built. They were sturdy and

geometrically sound. But the part of her that was her mother thought they were artless eyesores. She'd given no thought at all to style. To compensate, she built a parapet with evenly spaced crenels, and elaborate corbels in a gothic style. She dug into the walls and made a sweeping colonnade, thinking of Bernini's in St. Peter's.

For half an hour, she obsessed with perfecting the castle. She was on another world, and all she could think about was minutiae and artistic flaws, and the need to make it perfect and solid, but also to make it beautiful.

A bright flash made Susan look up. Arkushanangarushashutu glared down at her, crimson now, as if growing angry. Mother and Father approached. Their grey golem skin did not show any of the redness of cheek or wetness of eyes that usually accompanied their arguments.

"I've given the signal," Father said. "We should join the others." He looked at the sandcastle, and said nothing.

"You've gotten yourself dirty," Mother said, eyeing her disapprovingly.

"It's just a golem, Mom."

They turned and started down the beach towards the shareholders. Susan followed.

As the sun died, Father gave a speech that Susan did not hear, and Mother surreptitiously tried to brush wet sand from her backside. Arkushanangarushashutu boiled with dark spots. It bulged oddly as if hollow, and belched tendrils of itself into space. Susan realized it had died already. That she was seeing eight light minutes into the past. It was too late to change anything.

Susan looked back at the sandcastle. She desperately wanted to leave the group, to dash across the beach and kick it, spit on it, ruin it in some way. In the light of the dying sun, she saw the castle contained nothing of herself. But it was too late.

All around her, people were making sounds of awe. "Here it comes," Father said.

And just before her sandcastle turned to glass, Susan watched the sun explode.

ABOUT THE AUTHOR

Micah Hyatt began writing novels and short stories at the age of sixteen. It would be over a decade before he wrote anything worth reading. To pay the bills, he found work as a train conductor, a soldier, a hay baler, a dishwasher, a railroad safety liaison, and many other mundane jobs. Through it all, he never stopped writing.

His favourite books are those that take him to fantastic new places, and show underdogs overcoming their difficulties.

GOOD TO GO

Vaughan Stanger

After spending nearly thirty years managing the construction of the world's first space elevator, I was determined to participate in the inaugural ascent from the floating platform off Kourou. Still in my prime thanks to antiaging treatments, I felt as strong and healthy as any astronaut, even though my presence on the crew was mostly for show. The risks were low, or so my AI advisor informed me. Spun from carbon nanotubes and reeled downwards from a small asteroid captured by Planetary Resources Inc. in the late 2030s, nothing could disrupt that ribbon; nothing physical, at any rate.

As I took my place in the up-capsule, I mulled over the many false starts I'd witnessed. There would be no more pullback to low Earth orbit; no more "we can't afford to do it"; no more reality TV show nonsense. As New Year 2076 dawned, the long-postponed Big Push into the solar system could finally begin.

We were good to go.

The seven-day journey to Upside gave me plenty of time to perfect my speech about building the plasma-drive shuttles that would transport us onwards. But the greeting I received from the station's AI when I floated into the control room gave me one hell of a shock.

< Go back and tidy your room! >

The Upside AI's message reverberated in my head while I executed a slow, 360-degree rotation, as if it inhabited the walls.

"Pardon?"

< Go back and … >

"Okay, okay. I heard you the first time!"

A call to Downside revealed that most of their systems had just gone offline. Here at Upside, only comms and life support remained operational, along with the down-capsule's controls.

Since the Upside AI declined to respond to any further questions, my team and I were left with no choice except to return the way we'd come. It was an inglorious retreat, to say the least.

That was just the beginning.

• • •

Shortly after we began our descent, news arrived from Downside that every inhabited orbital facility was to be evacuated with immediate effect, since their AIs had also demonstrated noncompliance. Seemingly, humankind had been locked out of *all* its spaceside operations, not just the El.

Furthermore, < Tidy your room! > had gone global, with every adult inhabitant on the planet receiving a culturally appropriate translation. What I'd witnessed in geostationary orbit was the advent of Singularity, or as one of the few remaining human journalists named it: Sumkind. Most human experts had placed the onset of Singularity at least two decades into the future, making it the AI equivalent of practical nuclear fusion.

So much for predictions!

At least the terrifying visions depicted in the movies and virts hadn't come to pass. Most of our computers and AIs continued to work perfectly well. The main exceptions were those required to control the El and inhabited spacecraft, or to launch weapons of mass destruction. I heard some reports about problems with automated oil wells and coal mines but I dismissed those as being of no particular concern to me.

After decades of speculation about what our electronic offspring might do to us when they grew up we'd found out that they behaved more like Mary Poppins than the Terminator.

Unsurprisingly, most of us reacted like children.

• • •

Now, I wasn't stupid; I did understand what

Sumkind meant by "tidy your room." But I didn't regard the environmental consequences of man-made climate change as my problem to solve. The United Nations had established a plethora of commissions and conventions for that purpose. *Good luck with that*, I muttered whenever I heard about the latest last-best-hope initiative.

"Not my battle," I told a reporter who pressed me on the point. To my way of thinking, I was working towards a goal that transcended terrestrial concerns.

It's a pity I didn't realise that Sumkind's riffing on my privileged upbringing was a message targeted *specifically* at me.

No one ever got away with calling me stupid, but I'd certainly aced the exams in naivety. My husband said much the same thing before I divorced him.

Anyhow, the people who paid my salary wanted solutions that would get us off Earth.

At first, I focussed my team on regaining control of the El. No way was Space Mom—as my kids continued to call me even now that they had kids of their own—going to let a bunch of AIs deny us affordable access to the solar system.

Needless to say, we tried switching our computers off and on again, but Sumkind had distributed its core capabilities with commendable rigour. Combatting a massively networked conspiracy proved impossible, as some tiny part of it infested every electronic device on the planet—and beyond it, too. Sumkind didn't fry us with particle beams because it didn't need to. Following each futile reboot, it let us carry on with our lives pretty much as before.

In the meantime, the world got even hotter. With dozens of coastal cities swamped because the Antarctic ice shelves had collapsed, not to mention vital food chains unravelling in the rapidly acidifying oceans, you'd think I'd have taken the hint. But no, what I as poster girl for the "take it back" movement focussed on was how to engineer our way out of Earth's gravity well.

It seemed like we'd won a victory when my team figured out how to get the El working under manual control. I watched in horror as their latest brainchild got stuck twenty miles up as a result of transverse oscillations. We had one hell of a job getting our volunteers down again.

< Tidy your room! >

Not to be thwarted, my team assembled a rocket launcher to put a manned capsule in orbit, again without the use of computers. It was like a throwback to the 1950s, complete with rockets exploding thirty seconds after take-off. Volunteer astronauts soon became a thing of the past.

< Tidy your room! >

Sumkind's message never changed. Neither did my team's response, at least initially. They kept on dreaming up new ways to finesse the rules, none of which worked for long. Finally we flat ran out of ideas.

By then, the world really needed something done, as the ever-growing list of abandoned cities and failed harvests attested. Despite the urgency of the situation, proceedings at the United Nations dragged on for a *long* time before they got around to cross-examining me.

"I assume you understand what 'tidy your room' means?"

"I'm sure everyone does." Eager to show I was a right-thinking person, I added, "Collectively, we have to sort out things here on Earth before Sumkind will let us off it again."

"So why aren't you helping to achieve that?"

"I manage space projects."

My personal AI informed me that my shrug did not play well with the global audience.

"Don't you find that frustrating, given the current situation?"

I nodded. "Yeah, you could say that."

"Would you agree then that any competent manager could deliver our satellite renewal program?"

Failed communications and remote-sensing satellites needed replacing of course, so that the powers-that-be could conduct their endless debates about how to avert climate Armageddon. Ever obliging, Sumkind let us launch the necessary rockets.

"Yes," I said.

That was the moment Sumkind caught me: hook, line, and sinker.

"Okay, here's the thing. We urgently need you to refocus your skills on terrestrial projects, so that humankind won't *need* to escape from Earth."

It was not so much a request as an order, one which was witnessed by an audience of billions.

How could I refuse?

So that's how Space Mom became Earth Mom.

• • •

I'm not going to pretend that saving the planet was easy, but it helped that we knew what needed doing. Even more importantly, the UN had finally persuaded the wealthier nations to implement a funding regime that enabled us to get on with the *how*. Sadly, not everyone toed the line. Millions continued to die in futile wars, despite Sumkind restraining our trigger fingers when it came to the really dirty stuff. Bullets, bombs, and napalm still worked fine, as the residents of Delhi, Seoul, and Washington, D.C. learned the hard way. I suppose Sumkind must have reckoned that every little bit helped.

Confirmation that we were on the right track came when Sumkind's message to me changed.

< Do not come up until your room is tidy. >

Yes, nanny.

But in any event, I was too busy to think more

than casually about resuming space exploration. The global to-do list seemed never-ending. *Practical* nuclear fusion; solar power from self-assembled space mirrors; CO_2 fixing in sedimentary rocks; hydrogen generation from bacterial cracking of methane; ocean plankton reseeding; planting GM rainforests; synthesizing proteins for human consumption—pretty much every credible proposal contributed to the cure. If anything, the diktats about birth rate, longevity, and consumption proved harder to make stick, but we got there in the end.

Unsurprisingly, the people needed someone to blame now that every gram of carbon they emitted and every calorie they consumed got deducted from their lifetime allowances. But I could cope with the brickbats, or so I thought.

Unfortunately, despite my personal AI's best efforts, word had got out that not only was I *still* taking antiaging drugs, which had long since been banned, but also that I'd negotiated a permanent exemption from the emicon limits. To me, these arrangements seemed perfectly fair given that my job required me to provide a firm hand on the tiller while scanning the horizon for new risks. Which just goes to show that privilege wears blinkers.

Hence the gun held to my head, live on prime time.

"What do you want me to do?" I said between

whimpers.

"We *require* you to watch your grandchildren die."

Terror struck me dumb until I realised what my captor really meant.

"So I get to carry on?"

"That's right, Earth Mom. But you are the *only* exception."

It was a lot better than getting a bullet in the head, which was the fate of everyone else who'd made the same arrangements as me.

All things considered, I did pretty well out of this *fait accompli*. Two of my grandchildren even became parents, thanks to their super-useful genes.

But the demands of my job left me with little time to dote on the younger members of my tribe.

Ninety-nine years were to pass before I rode the El again.

• • •

To be frank, I'd been expecting to receive permission for at least ten years. The global temperature graph had peaked in 2165 and the oceans were beginning to deacidify. Conditions remained horrendous in the tropics, but even the most trenchant of pessimists could see that we'd turned a corner. The world was healing, albeit slowly. We were getting there.

I'd sent messages.

We've tidied our room.

And:

We promise not to mess it up again.
Finally a reply thundered in my head.
< Come on up, Earth Mom. >
Even Sumkind called me that.

• • •

Viewed from geostationary orbit, everything on Earth looked remarkably serene. The tropics presented cotton-candy clouds aplenty but hardly any hurricanes or typhoons. New patches of green confirmed the rebirth of the Amazon rainforest. From this vantage point I couldn't pick out any of our undersea cities, but I knew they were there.

< What do you intend to do next? >
True to my long-suppressed instincts, I called up an image of Mars on the nearest screen. Needless to say, I still felt that old pang. I imagined myself planting boot prints on Martian soil before throwing the switch on a terraforming project. Well, okay, those probably wouldn't be *my* boots, but hey, a great-great-grandmother could dream, right?

"Humankind needs another home. We've learned the hard way that if we put all our eggs in one basket —"

I didn't get the chance to develop my analogy any further.

< Go home, Earth Mom. >
I waved my hands towards the screen displaying the earth. "Oh, come on! What's the problem now?"

< You have not changed enough. >

"Seriously? Look what we've achieved! We've learned to walk before we try to run. We've changed how we think about our home."

< That is only the first step. >

My attempts to probe further got me nowhere. Evidently, Sumkind had no intention of explaining what the next step, or steps, might involve.

Go home and figure it out, I muttered to myself.

I had plenty to ponder while I rode the down-capsule back to Kourou.

• • •

It took an official visit to sub-Belize-02 for the necessary insight to emerge from the surf of daily distraction.

The last of my Damascene moments occurred one month after my return from Upside, while I watched the antics of one of my great-great-great-grandsons through an inch of toughened plastic. I was thinking that fins and gills suited Stefan just fine when he dribbled out a greeting composed of bubbles. Emulating Sumkind, my translator fed its interpretation straight into my head.

Hey, Earth Mom!

"Good to see you Stefan." I didn't bother adding the string of numbers and letters that indicated his lineage, baseline configuration, and subsequent mods.

Dive right in—the water's lovely!

It was kind of him to offer, but subaqua never really appealed to me. Different strokes for different folks, I reckoned. Now, if he'd been suggesting rod-and-line off the stern of a yacht, like in that photo my grandpa took of me … Ah well, those were the days.

Stefan's next bubble stream translated as:

Keep on sticking it to Sumkind.

I loved the way my translator turned gibber-fish into phrases only I would understand.

Dutiful as always, I promised Stefan I would do so. Not that I'd figured out what Sumkind actually wanted from me yet.

Then, as I watched Stefan swim off into the deep blue haze, I slapped my forehead so hard my vision blurred momentarily.

You have not changed enough.

That was it. Stefan and his peers were showing us the way. If our species was ever to head out into the solar system for keeps, we'd have to modify ourselves to suit the territory, not terraform the territory to suit ourselves.

My next speech to a worldwide audience went down no better than its predecessors. On the plus side, they didn't vote for my termination, mainly out of respect for my age. Being unique had its advantages.

"Now we've improved conditions on Earth, some of us are eager to move on." I shook my head like a school principal disappointed by her students' behaviour. "But Sumkind will only let us do that when it's *sure* we won't repeat our previous mistakes. If we're going to inhabit the solar system, we have to apply the lessons we've learned on Earth.

"Yes, we *have* tidied our room, but that doesn't mean we get to foul up someone else's, whether that someone is a microbe or a sentient being. If we want to move on, we have to change ourselves first."

Most of the world's two billion inhabitants shrugged and went back to coping with the demands of living in a recuperating ecosystem, while a few visionary types began experimenting with some really out-there mods. True to form, I returned to project managing. There was plenty to do.

• • •

Thirty years passed before Sumkind called me again.

< Come on up, Space Mom! >

Sometimes I felt like Sumkind used the El as a fishing line, baiting me with the prospect of other worlds to explore, while I harassed the human race into doing the right thing.

One last time, I told myself.

• • •

When I arrived at Upside, I found the base running on automatic. Sumkind had departed, as my call to Downside quickly confirmed. Its farewell gift to us was a virt depicting a laser-pushed nanocraft heading out of the ecliptic. We'd been left to our own devices, with no rules to follow except those we imposed on ourselves.

Good to go at last.

Predictably, some folk reverted to the old ways as soon as the stabilisers came off. Everyone thinks they know why the Green Mars colony suffered a lethal ecocollapse in 2225. Those vids were faked, I'm afraid. But most people got the message. The rules were here to stay.

Not long after my return to Earth, I petitioned the powers-that-be to let me stop taking the antiaging drugs. They agreed I'd done my penance. I'd reached the point where I craved some certainty in my life. Now that I have it, I wish I didn't. But that's life, I guess.

Still, it looks like I'll be leaving something worthwhile behind.

Four members of my tribe are out there now, working on, or more accurately under, the solar system's minor planets and moons. Jedro has settled on Ceres, where he's investigating the microbes found in the salt water percolating beneath the dwarf planet's crust. Mila-Mila* have put down roots in the ooze at the bottom of Europa's ocean, where they're breeding ripple-worms the size of the Titanic. Olva is breathing ethane while free diving in one of Titan's lakes. Unfortunately, hir tail flicks didn't translate well enough for me to comprehend the precise nature of hir project.

And only yesterday, I received a virt from Wanda, who's currently in transit to Pluto. She's getting spliced with her crewmate Nomi. I've sent my congratulations. Better still, it appears my Space Mom tendencies have passed along the line. I understand they'll be building a *really* big laser to push our sail-ships beyond the solar system.

When their descendants dive into the ocean of a world orbiting another star, I trust they'll remember the lessons we learned. We must fit in, not foul up.

Maybe they'll encounter Sumkind out there. If so, I hope they'll ask why it didn't stick around. I like to think its absence is intended as a message: an invitation to swim in deeper oceans, maybe.

< Come on in, the interstellar medium is lovely! >

I won't live long enough to hear the answer, but I hope some of my descendants will.

Wherever they end up, I hope the fishing is good.

ABOUT THE AUTHOR

Formerly an astronomer and more recently a research project manager in a defence and aerospace company, Vaughan Stanger now writes science fiction and fantasy full time. Nevertheless, he still craves that holiday on the moon he was promised as a child. His stories have appeared in *Daily Science Fiction*, *Abyss & Apex*, *Postscripts*, *Nature Futures*, and *Interzone*. He has published two collections, *Moondust Memories* and *Sons of the Earth & Other Stories*, which are available as ebooks and print-on-demand paperbacks, and is hard at work on a series of SF novels. Follow Vaughan's writing adventures at www.vaughanstanger.com and @VaughanStanger.

DARK MOON

Liam Hogan

"Do you see it?" hissed Gramps, bony fingers digging into my shoulder.

"See *what*?" I said, trying to shrug him off.

"The moon, boy! The moon!"

I rolled my eyes. Everyone knew you couldn't see the moon. Not anymore, anyway. Not without a special lens at the end of a telescope, the features picked out in flickering green, the next kid in line trying to push you out of the way. Even then you only got a good look on the clearest of nights, when the city light didn't reflect back off the clouds, washing out the stars.

No one could see the moon with the naked eye. Least of all Gramps, who couldn't read without glasses as thick as the old books he collected. Mostly, he used an app to read things for him. It was simpler that way.

I wondered if he was getting senile. Gramps was so ancient he says he remembers the moon before the Darkening. Says some nights it hung in the sky like a great white balloon.

I've seen the pictures. They're not all that. How could they be when a full moon was 400,000 times dimmer than the sun, even *before* we tampered with it?

The Darkening is pretty much the first science lesson we get taught. The teachers come back to it every year, expanding on the problems the earth faced, drilling into us how it took the whole world to agree to change.

I guess it's important to them.

It's a bit of a bore though, the third or fourth time around.

Way back when everybody twigged that the issue wasn't *proving* global warming—because that had very much already proved itself—that instead we had to do something about it, this Mexican woman—not even a scientist, a *politician*—broke it down as simply as it needed to be for everyone to finally understand.

The temperature of the surface of the earth— where we all lived—depended on three things, she said:

How much light came from the sun.

How much we reflected back.

And how much heat was generated on Earth.

Simple, right? Hard to believe people used to fight over it.

With global temperatures undeniably rising, what could we do to stop it? What could we do to lessen the terrible storms, the rising sea levels, and everything else we'd caused?

We couldn't do much about the sun. It blazed away pretty steadily with only a small wobble over its eleven-year sunspot cycle.

The energy the earth generated was mostly low level radioactivity. Plus us. Burning forests—prehistoric or otherwise—generated heat, though it's what that did to the atmosphere that really counted. The albedo (that's a fancy term for the reflectivity of the earth) was how we got into trouble in the first place. Greenhouse gases decreased it: more of the sun's light got trapped and so of *course* temperatures went up.

Back then, despite the warning signs that had been around for ages, the process was accelerating. Snow was bright and shiny and the rock or ocean hidden beneath was not. Ninety percent reflective, versus six percent. So as the glaciers and ice caps melted away, things got warmer still.

There was talk of painting the Alps white. Discussions of whether solar panels were actually a bad thing, since they were designed to absorb as much light as possible. Talk of putting up a great big shiny satellite to reflect some of the sun's rays away, casting a shadow over a desert or maybe across the sea.

Then someone suggested darkening the moon.

It seemed crazy at the time. The moon, according to the scientists, was pretty dark already. Darker than

Gramps says it was, anyway. It only reflected—and this is a number everyone knows, once they start school—twelve percent of the light of the sun, over its monthly phases.

Plus, it's a long way from the earth. The boffins calculated that the moon gives out one ten-thousandth of the energy of the sun and most of that not even in visible light.

Though as NASA pointed out, if you *really* wanted a satellite to tinker with, why not use one that was already there?

As geoengineering projects go, it had one major advantage over the other crazy schemes that were being suggested: it wasn't on Earth, so the cure wasn't likely to be worse than the disease.

It's not the only thing our parents and grandparents did. The last chunk of coal was burnt fifty years ago and they've been extracting carbon *back* from the atmosphere ever since.

A lot of it ended up on the moon.

The "painting" was simple enough. Just void the carbon dust into space around our lunar companion and the black particles would slowly rain down. I suppose we only needed to paint one side, but it turned out easier to do both.

Over a decade, so the teachers tell us, the moon faded away to nothing. From twelve percent down to a little less than one. Through the school telescope, you can see the occasional white splodge—the crater of a recent meteorite—but carbon is still raining down, so I guess the splodges will get softened back into the dark.

The moon was still there, tugging at the earth, creating the tides. Every so often things lined up just so and we'd get a solar eclipse. But you don't see it before and you don't see it after.

The scientific jury was still out as to whether it'd done much good, but it was a pretty powerful symbol at the time.

A bit less so, for anyone who grew up never having seen the moon. Or at least, not directly.

Gramps suddenly pointed up into the night sky. I'd been thinking about my homework, thinking how cold it was getting, thinking about whether my parents would let me stay up late because Gramps was here.

"There!" he wheezed.

Where he was pointing, my eyes now used to the dark, there was a dim red glow. A blood-red penny in the sky.

"What ...?" I gaped.

"The moon!"

"But it's red?"

He grinned, spun me around. In the dark, I couldn't see his face, but I felt his warm breath on my cheek. "A lunar eclipse! The moon is sitting in the shadow of the earth. The sunlight is red because it's going through our atmosphere, our polluted atmosphere. And the moon—the moon still reflects a little of the longer wavelengths."

We stood and watched in awe until a cloud blocked the ghostly red light, until the house lights flicked back on and Mum called us in for cocoa and cookies.

At the kitchen table I bit a crescent from the pale oat circle, nibbled at it until it was only a thumbnail wide, glad to be warm, but thinking about that dark red disc.

Long term—much, much longer term than any politicians were thinking—the sun was gradually warming, as it fused hydrogen into helium. Growing fat in its old age, as well. Future scientists—who may or may not be human—might one day have to drag the earth a bit further away from its life-giving and life-taking rays.

I wonder if we'll take the moon with us.

ABOUT THE AUTHOR

Liam Hogan is an Oxford Physics graduate and award-winning London-based writer. His short story "Ana" appears in *Best of British Science Fiction 2016* (NewCon Press) and his twisted fantasy collection *Happy Ending Not Guaranteed* is published by Arachne Press. Find out more at happyendingnotguaranteed.blogspot.co.uk, or tweet @LiamJHogan.

INTERVENTION

William Delman

I'm staring at my mother. "What do you mean you're not leaving?"

We had just spent three exhausting days emptying her house ahead of Hurricane Zara's impending landfall.

Every computer, piece of radio equipment, book, antique, scrap of clothing, and bit of sentimental bric-a-brac is in the moving truck behind me. The autodrive is patiently waiting for someone to key in the destination—my home on Lafayette Island in Salem, MA.

"You heard me. I'm staying." She smiles, serene as a clear blue sky. Her posture is relaxed, entirely comfortable in sweatpants and an ancient T-shirt emblazoned with two fading grapplers surrounded by the words "This is How I Roll."

Even at sixty-eight, she's still scalpel sharp and fit thanks to a near religious dedication to her Brazilian jujitsu classes, which is to say I can't write off her declaration as a sudden and suicidal cognitive failure.

"Stop joking." I laugh nervously. "We need to get out of here."

Long Beach Island—what's left of it after decades of rising seas—is almost completely deserted thanks to the apocalyptic mantras emanating from every meteorological service and government agency.

"No," she says. "*You* need to get out of here. I'm going to stay and see if I'm right about the aliens." She glances back toward the house and the massive satellite dish mounted to the roof.

"I'm sorry, you're what?" I stare at her. "What do you think they're going to do?"

She turns back and fixes me with her implacable glare. It's a look I'm deeply familiar with from adolescence and holiday conversations about questionable life choices. It isn't a good sign.

Humanity has been listening to signals from TESS-32 for five years, but according to the International Space Agency, the only things we've learned about the aliens is that they're carbon based, have very strange taste in music, and don't know anything more about the universe than we do.

A lot of people think TESS-32 is a hoax designed to keep the masses distracted while civilization collapses in plain sight.

Meanwhile, the Interventionists—many of whom have scientific backgrounds, like my mother—are convinced the aliens are already in the neighbourhood, ready and waiting to save us from ourselves.

Her beliefs have become a bit of a sticking point between us.

"Are you insane?" I cross my arms. "Everyone is running west like our idiot president announced a new Louisiana Purchase. The whole Mid-Atlantic region is making its peace. It's time to leave and get behind the MassBay Seawall, not go all in on some absurd theory."

"Hypothesis," my mother chides me. "Zara is exactly the kind of life-altering event that could force the Tess to reveal themselves. And I've been sending them signals."

I'm quaking with fatigue and frustration. "This Interventionist stuff … I mean, what if you're right? Can they instantly kill superstorms and sequester three centuries of aerosolized fossils? Or maybe they're going to pluck you from the flood like some extraterrestrial version of the Coast Guard?"

"Don't do that," she says. "Don't make fun."

"Listen, Mom, if the aliens show up, or don't, we'll have time to discuss it after we're safe."

She shakes her head, unhooks her canteen from her belt, pulls a bottle of pills from her pocket and swallows a tablet before smiling sadly.

This is something I've seen her do a lot over the last three days—both the sad smiling and pill popping. Now, she hands me the empty pill bottle. I read the label and recognize the drug from the last few years of my father's life.

It feels like the ground is vanishing under my feet. I try to imagine my mother, a woman who defines herself through activity and initiative, losing herself to body- and ego-shattering pain. What would I do if I was the one watching the tide roll in?

Dad always said I was too much like Mom—always ready to go through the next moment by myself just to prove I could—that I needed to be reminded I wasn't alone from time to time.

I hand her back the empty bottle. "Fine. If you're staying, so am I. The earth won't miss us."

"Well, if you're going to be like that." She scowls and takes a few steps toward the truck, but stops when I don't move. "Are we going?"

"Hold on." I say. "Just like that?"

"I'm too tired to fight. Lead the way, and I'll follow."

I turn around and start walking. That's when my small, old, fierce, sick mother jumps on my back and tries to sink in a rear naked choke.

"Ah! Seriously?" I get a hand between her forearm and my throat.

"I'm sorry my love, but I'm not losing myself, and I'm not taking you with me."

"Stop being crazy!" I drop into the turtle position and hear her grunt in surprise as I roll her gently over my shoulder.

"You've been training."

I come up to my feet, gasping. "Had to see what all the fuss was about. Seriously though, what was the plan? Choke me out and lift my unconscious body into the truck, then turn on the autodrive and send me on my way?"

"Pretty much." She shrugs.

"Do you know what I weigh?"

She looks me up and down. "I could get you up if I had to."

"Not a chance. Now stop trying to tap out, and get in the damn truck. Unless you think we should wait for Zara. I love you. It's your call."

After that neither of us says anything for a long time.

She breaks the silence after we're north of Hartford. "You really think I'm wrong? About the aliens, I mean."

I shrug. "Either way, you and Dad taught me we save ourselves, and we save each other. There are no magic solutions."

"You know," she says, "sometimes there are no solutions at all."

I don't know how to answer, but we keep moving.

ABOUT THE AUTHOR

William's work has previously appeared in *Little Blue Marble*, *The Arcanist*, and *Daily Science Fiction*. When he's not writing, William can often be found on Twitter at @DelmanWilliam, perusing the Codex forums, or on the mats at Fenix BJJ in West Peabody.

I WOULD LET YOU KNOW

Robert Dawson

(Golden Shovel,[1] after W. H. Auden)

It's serious, you know, but there's still time.
Caution's no crime. You'll act someday, you will.
"You could have done more still," whispers from the future say.
Ice slowly melts away, and you answer nothing.

Your car sits puffing at the traffic light but
it takes too long to shut off the engine. I
do the same, I will not lie, though we've been told
the air cannot hold our waste. The children ask you:
what did you do when you could? The seas are rising so.

ABOUT THE AUTHOR

Robert Dawson teaches mathematics at a Nova Scotian
university. His stories have appeared in *Nature Futures*, *AE*,
and numerous other periodicals and anthologies. He's an

alumnus of the Sage Hill and Viable Paradise writing workshops.

---

[1] About the form:

A "Golden Shovel" is a word-level telestich: the last words of each line form a quotation from another poem. Terrance Hayes, the inventor of the form, named it after the Gwendolyn Brooks poem that he quoted. Here, Dawson has used a line from W. H. Auden's "If I Could Tell You."

INVASIVE ALIEN SPECIES

Tris Matthews

In the diverse crowd all skin colours and sexes squeezed around one another to fill every inch of the seminar hall. Unblinking eyes shimmered in moist expectation as the professor took the stage. Known for his eccentricity as much as his vast intellect, he began by extracting a pair of extinct spectacles from the age of short-sightedness and jamming them atop his bulbous snout. In a voice of rich and varied tones, he addressed his audience.

"There was an old lady who swallowed a fly;
I don't know why she swallowed a fly—
perhaps she'll die.

"In CE 2003 the alien species *Harmonia axyridis* was first recorded in the British Isles. Originating in Asia, this invasive species—known commonly as the harlequin ladybird—was purposefully brought to thirteen European countries to prevent aphids and scale insects exploiting the endless fields of homogeneous crops that replaced natural ecosystems. Invasive alien species are known threats to global biodiversity. Though that is, self-evidently, a tautology.

"To catch the fly, she swallowed a spider
that wriggled and jiggled and tickled inside her.

"There were forty-three native species of ladybird prior to the harlequin invasion. To be sure, just like the spread of Christianity—or, later, capitalism—the less aggressive species weren't violently wiped out; they were simply consistently outperformed in the race for resources. Not only did the native species not know what hit them, the harlequins that did the hitting didn't know they'd been the hitters! As a curious side note, a further danger of the harlequin was another little beast residing inside it—a microsporidian parasite to which the harlequin was immune but British ladybirds fall foul.

"To catch the spider, she swallowed a bird.
How absurd to swallow a bird!

"Biodiversity! What is it? If it looks and acts like a ladybird, does it matter if it's one species or forty-three? Example one: temperature rises, clouds vaporise, more sunlight reaches our planet, and those ladybird species with fewer spots survive because their lighter coating reflects more electromagnetic radiation, and vice versa for the darker bugs in cooler times. Example two: penicillin was discovered by accident from a species of mould that appeared on a serendipitously uncovered Petri dish. Such incidents are far from unique—different species solve problems in different ways, so reduction in biodiversity means reduction in serendipity. Did the people of the time bear such examples in mind?

"To hunt down the bird, she swallowed a cat.
Imagine that—swallowed a cat!

"Scientists took notice. They didn't stop it—preventative measures had to be implemented by governments, who were controlled by people, who were convinced they were powerless—but they did describe, monitor, and model the spread. So did the general population know or care? Of course they did—the harlequin proved to be mildly bothersome in its tendency to roost in houses in the colder months and ooze a rather revolting aroma. Moreover, its proclivity for grape vines led to an unpleasant tinge of acidity in the taste of local wines.

"To follow the cat, she swallowed a dog.
Oh what a hog, to swallow a dog!

"Therefore, to eradicate the bug they'd imported to exterminate aphids, that hosted the microsporidian that killed all the natives—they developed harlequin-targeting sexually transmitted mites, thinking the best weapon to fight the blight was a blight for the blight. As *we* well know, this kind of solution only leads to more resistant strains of the offending beast, *and* risks infection of related species, which is exactly what happened. *Apis mellifera*—the faithful honeybee, already near the brink due to neonicotinoids and habitat loss—were decimated. That's when they brought in the mice (*Mus musculus*—themselves an invasive alien species, though aren't we all?)

"There was an old lady who swallowed a goat;
she just opened her throat and swallowed that goat.

"The mice had a literal field day. They gorged and bred, substantially reducing *H. axyridis* populations, as desired. However, with their increased numbers and the sudden shortage of ladybirds, they hunted other foods, thereby double-whammying those poor species already negatively impacted by the modified mites. Not ones to learn from their mistakes, the people of the time engineered foxes whose pups would be sterile. An intriguing idea, and it would have been scientifically valuable to observe how *that* ended, but then we arrived.

> *"To displace the goat, she swallowed a cow!*
> *I don't know how she swallowed a cow.*

"Life is sparse in this universe, but where it develops, it tirelessly bootstraps its way up till it is smart enough to perform autogenocide—in all known cases except our own. Though we'd observed the ruins of life on so many planets, here was our first chance to encounter aliens *before* they devoured themselves. We *had* to meet our neighbours so we could all coexist peacefully in this wide void. They didn't trust us, and demanded we prove our good intentions by feeding them knowledge and solutions, starting with the problem of *Harmonia axyridis.*

> *"There was an old lady who swallowed a horse;*
> *…she died, of course.*

"Long story short, we *did* solve all the natives' problems. They came to respect, trust, love, and depend on us. Those few of our ancestors who had braved the long journey here lived among *Homo sapiens* as teachers, then friends and equals for five centuries; fitting in, thriving, multiplying … right up until the *Homo sapiens* died out. Initially, we didn't notice their dwindling numbers, then we tried our best to reverse the trend, but in vain. Incidentally, the ladybirds we've seen so many of this summer—they are the infamous harlequins. You see, once an invasive alien species has a foothold, they are nigh impossible to dislodge."

ABOUT THE AUTHOR

Tris Matthews lives in London and works as a data curator for a scientific publisher. He is occasionally inspired to fiction by the data he curates. "Invasive Alien Species" was such a case. It's also one of the first stories he managed to plan in its entirety before beginning writing, and thus quite a milestone for him. Follow his progress at trismatthews.com and @tori_tris.

SEEDLESS

D. A. Xiaolin Spires

<u>Seedless Watermelon and Imaginary Spices</u>
Cut and cube seedless watermelon.
Add a dash of seedless peppercorns.
Sprinkle with seedless sesame seeds.
Serve cold, preferably in a glass bowl.

• • •

First it was the summer fruit. Watermelons, grapes, all seedless for the convenience of eaters and possible chokers. Grandma Chen loved it. She never liked swallowing seeds and never liked digging her fingers into the cold flesh to remove them.

But eventually Grandma Chen wondered where all the seeds were disappearing off to.

Even after she became gastronome extraordinaire and head chef at a Michelin-starred restaurant (sought for her expertise in the regional specialties of Chinese cuisine), she used to take a few weeks off in the summer and leave her work to her sous chef. It was during these weeks that she would join her daughters in a summer game. She would contact her produce supplier and they would stock up on summer melons and other sun-gorged fruit. Then, they would hold their very own summer "Fruit Fling Olympics," contests her kids invented on the backyard porch, taking bites and spitting, to see who could eject them the farthest onto flowerbeds. Her second daughter Yiting performed especially beautiful arcs, flights of black watermelon seeds that landed in perfect parabolas onto petals, leaves, and dirt.

But this innocent family challenge in time became obsolete with the advent of fruits without seeds.

After the watermelon and grapes, the next in the lineup of seed-vacant fruits were oranges, cherries, and kiwis.

The strawberry, pale with the lack of its black freckles, was the most appalling aesthetic abomination, thought Grandma Chen. She ripped off its leafy head and let the naked berry sit in a pool of clotted cream and lotus paste.

• • •

In Chinatown, wax apples, custard apple, lychee, and pomegranates held out. All the other supermarkets in Grandma Chen's vicinity had converted, displaying red signs with logos of a smiling boy in a bowl haircut biting into a coreless apple to flag the new range of crop specimens. But in Chinatown, seed lovers still found willing vendors, a market for a shrinking minority.

Only last year at A-Bing's stand in the open-air market did Grandma Chen start seeing seedless custard apples. She brought them back home in a handmade basket. Leaning over the marble counter, she scooped out the discrete bits of sweetness from the green spiky skin. The inner flesh moved around like mush, without the internal architecture of seeds to hold it in place.

Like rice congee, she thought. *Pork marrow or duck brains.* She put her lips against the white flesh and took one juicy bite. Her exquisite sense of taste told her there was something missing, a feeling left unresolved on her tongue.

• • •

Once they exhausted the fruits, the breeders moved to other produce: squashes and pumpkins, olives and peppers.

For her *baobei* Chialing's birthday, Grandma Chen bought a luscious red bell pepper to accent her celebratory pulled noodles. With her carving knife in hand, the slit she made opened up to an empty cavity, divested of white teardrop specks.

She grabbed the silver teaspoon she had ready for scooping and rested it back in the drawer. She pushed the drawer to a close, marvelling at the strange crimson variety she held in her palm. Then, she used her deft hands to slice thin wedges.

I guess this saves time, she thought, picturing the

hollow pocket when she split the bell pepper in half. Her business acumen told her it would also save labour and thus money for the restaurant. What she found jarring was that emptiness, the space that once held an abundance, the source for her spring garden.

She held up her cut bell pepper slices in the sunlight streaming through the kitchen window and peered at the translucent red skin.

She thought of the dense fresh dirt in her garden bed and went online to find seeds, only to discover that single-generation sorts were the only option for purchase.

• • •

Soon, potatoes no longer had eyes, just smooth skins that peeled with a flourish. Corn still had seeds, though, Grandma thought with relief, as she husked and chiseled a few ears, sprinkling on a cocktail of rubs and pastes to marinate, for a modern take on egg drop soup.

It was a rainy, cold March night. She visualized flavours interlacing into a zesty net, the kind of sprightly brightness that could chase out grey clouds. It was just the thing that she needed to spice up her spring menu. At least her ears of corn would be brimming with aromatic seasonings. These were the ears of corn that still held out, that still displayed their proud seeds, pockets of juicy gusto popping in every bite.

After Grandma Chen was done with adding more care to the soup, she lifted up her wine glass set precariously on the counter edge and said, "To the obstinate *zea mays*, may you always rise up with seeds."

She picked off one of the yellow kernels and popped it into her mouth, her adept taste buds sauntering through the savoury journey and performing necessary evaluations.

• • •

But innovation never ceases to rest.

Soon frogs in pet stores no longer laid any eggs.

When Grandma replaced the hens in her coop from the fox incident, she found her yellow-feathered fowl deposited no eggs in their nests. Reproduction of crops and then pets became the intellectual property of the seller, its fate no longer resting in the hands of the consumer.

• • •

A steady diet of oolong tea, fish, produce, and tofu and Grandma Chen was still alive to see the birth of the fourth generation. Grandma Chen kept looking for the bulge that would hint at the coming of her great-grandchild. It was to her surprise that her *baobei* Chialing came bowling into her apartment in ballerina flats waving a brochure and holding onto her wife's arm. Both shared a wide smile.

"This one," said Chialing, pointing.

Grandma Chen looked at the folded brochure in

her granddaughter's hand. Opened to page 16. It was a photo of a black-haired baby with half-closed eyes, curled up in the fetal position.

"Dr. Geetha Vishwakarma and her team are growing her now," said Chialing. "We can pick her up in a week."

Grandma Chen remembered the name from an earlier conversation she only half paid attention to while she was thinking up the banquet menu for her own retirement party. At the time Grandma Chen was making a mental note of the ingredient purveyors. She was always in control of the technical aspects of food prep, always with all details in her grasp. Just because it was her own retirement party didn't mean she would forfeit her charge and let someone else take over. But there was something important about that conversation if only she could recall it.

Genetics obstetrician—that was it. Chialing had said that in reference to this doctor, the syllables now ringing in her ears. Grandma Chen wished she had followed up with more questions then.

She glanced through the attributes listed on the page, numbers that suggested a propensity for certain personality traits and statistics like expected growth rate and potential allergies.

She would likely be shy, but with keen intelligence, with a 46% possibility of a peanut allergy, Grandma Chen read. Then, with her thumb, Grandma Chen flicked through the pages of the brochure quickly, like a flip book, letting the different traits of the many cultivated babies ready for plucking settle upon her eyes.

Grandma Chen returned to the page she had held in place with her forefinger, and ran her hand over the image of the tiny *baobao*, her great-grandchild. She felt the gloss of the brochure in delicate strokes, as if she was running over the smooth skin of her own distended belly when she gave birth to her first child. It felt like a lifetime ago.

She was no longer simply Grandma, but Great-Grandma.

Staring at the teeny babe in the photo, Great-Grandma Chen couldn't help but think of the first altered watermelon she had bought from the supermarket decades ago, so devoid of tiny black seeds. She then recalled an earlier memory—sitting on the porch in the hot afternoon, eight months pregnant with her third child, spitting black seeds out into the grass, laughing with her two elder kids.

The black beady eyes of the child printed before her, so seed-like, rendered in so many pixels, stared back at her—the future progeny of her grandchild, the continuation of her family line.

ABOUT THE AUTHOR

D. A. Xiaolin Spires steps into portals and reappears in sites such as Hawai'i, NY, various parts of Asia, and elsewhere, with her keyboard appendage attached. Her work appears or is forthcoming in publications such as *Clarkesworld, Analog, Strange Horizons, Nature, Terraform, Uncanny, Grievous Angel, Fireside, Galaxy's Edge, StarShipSofa, Andromeda Spaceways* (Year's Best Issue), *Diabolical Plots, Factor Four, Toasted Cake, Pantheon, Outlook Springs*, ROBOT DINOSAURS, *Shoreline of Infinity,* LONTAR, *Mithila Review, Reckoning, Issues in Earth Science, Liminality, Star*Line, Polu Texni, Argot, Eye to the Telescope, Liquid Imagination, Little Blue Marble, Story Seed Vault,* and anthologies of the strange and beautiful: *Deep Signal, Ride the Star Wind, Sharp and Sugar Tooth, Broad Knowledge, Future Visions* and *Battling in All Her Finery*. Select stories can be read in German, Vietnamese, Estonian and French translation. She can be found on Twitter at @spireswriter and on her website: daxiaolinspires.wordpress.com.

BEAR #178

Holly Schofield

The scientists put the metal box in my brain for a reason. They are wise and clever and I'm sure the reason must be a good one.

Now, three campers face me on the trail just outside Banff. The tall one, a male, shows his teeth. When I was just a regular grizzly bear, I thought that meant aggression but now I know it means fear. The damp spot on the front of his hiking shorts confirms that.

The female person addresses the male. "Gordie, it's okay," she says. "It's Bear 178, the enhanced one. See the scar by her right ear?" She makes a pawing motion like scraping berries off a bush. "Go home, bear."

I am puzzled because I am already home.

The littlest camper smells of hamburgers. I would like to taste her face. The box in my head fizzes, like snowmelt bubbling through moss. That means, if I taste her face, I will be captured and killed.

"You can find food higher up in the Rockies," the one called Gordie tells me. "Head north." He points up the mountain where the glacier used to be.

I am proud that they are treating me like I am smart. Like I am a person.

Perhaps I am meant to act like one.

I stand up on my hind legs.

The people shriek like grey jays. The smell of urine grows stronger.

I thump down back on all fours and snort.

I am not a person. I am a bear.

I give a mighty roar. The campers turn and run down the path to the campground.

I follow.

The black surface of the parking lot hurts my foot pads. Beyond the campers cowering in their hot car, the garbage bins smell of deliciousness and rot.

A rusty spatula lies by the angled metal garbage cans with their bear-proof locks. I take the spatula in my paws and shove it under the clasp, releasing the catch. I shoulder the lid open. The delightful smell of burnt hotdogs wafts out.

My mother has taught me to eat only mushrooms, berries, and small mammals. I huff, remembering her wide face. A train struck her last winter as she licked up fallen wheat kernels on the tracks. I walked for an entire night before I found her body where it had been dragged, near one of the dark caves that the trains have dug into the mountains.

My empty stomach claws at my insides. Perhaps the scientists do not realize the mountain creeks have run dry and the bushes hold no fruit. But if I eat from this garbage can, my head will feel more than fizziness —it will burn like fire. I hesitate for a long time.

Finally, I let the lid fall and drop back to all fours. I am rewarded with a faint rush of apple-sweet happiness.

It does not last long.

And it does not feel as good as hotdogs taste.

I turn down one trail, then another. Everywhere are people. Everywhere is people food.

I snuffle and paw at my scar. The box in my head does not help me figure out where to go or how to find food. But, I realize, it has helped me figure out something else: the wise and clever scientists have enhanced my brain because they do not want to make hard decisions.

They want me to make them instead.

I head toward the setting sun.

The harsh smell of creosote hits my nose and I huff and snort. I follow the train tracks a long way, my claws clicking on gravel.

The sun is almost in the treetops when I hear a train rumble in the distance.

I stop on a railroad tie. The rumble grows louder.

I have made a decision: there is only one way to

avoid humans.

I lie down on the tracks and put my head on my paws.

This is how.

ABOUT THE AUTHOR

Holly Schofield travels through time at the rate of one second per second, oscillating between the alternate realities of city and country life. Her short stories have appeared in *Analog*, *Lightspeed*, *Escape Pod*, and many other publications throughout the world. She hopes to save the world through science fiction and homegrown heritage tomatoes. Find her at hollyschofield.wordpress.com.

THE COLOURS OF EUROPA, THE COLOURS OF HOME

Stewart C Baker

In the sea beneath Europa's thick and jagged layer of ice, all colours faded to a blue that was almost black. There was no green, no white, no blood-red stain of life ill spent. Nothing to remind Yihan of what she'd lost.

She stayed as long as she could in the submersible's remote interface, hunting out exotic microbes in the depths and shooting samples up to the surface, but each time she thought herself safe, the chirrup of the break timer sounded, bringing her back to Ling-Xian Station, four thousand metres above Europa's icy crust.

One day, she told herself, it would be different. One day she would swim on forever, become a Europan globefish and hunt her regrets to extinction.

• • •

Yihan came awake with a gasp and a shiver. She had been dreaming of the seas again. Dreaming of freedom.

Bleary-eyed, she wiped the sweat from her body with a towel, stuck it back onto the suction valve on the station's wall, then hooked one foot through a floor strap and tugged herself into a clean uniform. All this in the semidarkness of her room's night-mode lighting.

After she was dressed, she turned to the interior bulkhead. "Wake," she said, blinking as her eyes adjusted to day mode. "Scopes. Surface and external."

The bulkhead flickered, then two separate feeds appeared on it, split down the centre by a line of the station's usual hospital white.

The first showed Conamara Chaos—its cracks and ridges spreading out and away into the distance. This came from the lander below them, a survey device in its own right now that it had drilled down through the kilometres of ice and deployed the submersible into the waters beneath. The second was shot from a cam outside Ling-Xian Station and showed the moon itself, backlit by Jupiter's ever-shifting clouds.

Yihan launched herself gently to the wall, brushed her hand against the ice of the Chaos. She did this every morning. It helped her to see what was down there, what she was swimming beneath.

Yuri and Asami were already in the commons module when she drifted through its doorway a few minutes later, Yuri eating rehydrated kelp-and-soy brats

—a lunch Yihan wished wasn't so familiar—while Asami sipped lukewarm chamomile tea through a straw.

"Evening," Asami greeted her.

"Good morning."

"It's afternoon," Yuri said with an exaggerated eye roll, finishing off their habitual joke.

Yihan couldn't help but smile. If it wasn't for her crewmates, she didn't know how she'd survive out here so far from home. They were the only thing about Ling-Xian she could bring herself to like, for all that the station was her ticket to Europa and its seas.

"There's a message for you on the 'caster," Yuri continued in his thick Russian accent.

Of course there was. Yihan pulled a roll and a tube of coffee from the cabinet, took a deep breath, then let it out slowly as she popped the seal on the coffee. "I'll check it later," she said. "Thanks."

The "morning" passed as usual: breakfast; three hours of resistance training (Asami joking with her for an hour of it before going off to bed with a half-heard "'Night."); another towel bath and uniform change; the usual tests on samples shot up to the station from the lander to see if they might produce any useful antibiotics, followed by reports and status updates for Mission Control back home.

It was only at Yuri's reminder over lunch (his dinner) that Yifan promised to check the 'caster before she went down to Europa.

• • •

What to say about the 'caster room?

Its lack of scopes, its too-white hospital walls. It reminded her of home, of everything she'd left behind. Everything she'd abandoned.

When she first arrived on the station, she'd hung a cheap scroll on one wall that showed a girl drawing water in a bright bamboo forest. It was a parting gift from her mother—"So you never forget where we came from."—but the contrast only made things worse.

She set it from her mind and powered up the 'caster. The device ran through its usual startup, its lights flickering into being before her, three-dimensional strands of twisting blue-white light the colour of Europan ice. Once that stabilized, she called up her message and the strands bent and danced to form the shape of Hesheng, her living daughter.

Hesheng with her innocent eyes, with the same trusting words as always: "We miss you, Mom. When will you come home?"

The question called up memories Yihan wanted to forget. Squalling twin daughters, years of sleepless nights as they grew older. Then, in primary school, the first signs of Xixi's sickness. Endless visits to Hangzhou First People's Hospital beneath the choking smog. Her mother's sing-song voice reciting her own mother's stories of the old days, when bamboo culms stretched, green and yellowish brown, into the clean blue sky above Anji's mountains.

And other memories, even worse. The bone-sharp white of hospital walls. The stink of bile and vomit, and splashes of blood far redder than blood had any right to be.

She listened to the rest of the 'cast: stories of Hesheng's friends at school—hard to believe she was already in secondary—of the latest round of rationing, of how they'd gone to visit Xixi's grave despite a sandstorm, just her and her grandmother. That, at least, was something—that Mom was there with Hesheng.

Still, the guilt lingered, the shame she'd felt since defending her PhD in exomycology. Or since shortly after, anyway. She'd returned home, brimming with pride, to find her mother's tears and news of Xixi's death. The hospital, the blood. So much blood.

Under it all—the guilt, the shame, in Hangzhou and on Ling-Xian both—that sensation of pressure in her chest, of burning in her throat. The thought, relentless, that she should have done more. Should have been there for her daughter instead of working on her research. Or worked on it harder. Found new and exotic antibiotics without leaving the planet, so she could have cured Xixi in time.

At least she could find them now. At least she

could cure other people's children.

She sent a reply to Hesheng, faking a smile, telling her daughter about a globefish she'd spotted the day before, about the latest advance Asami had made on Yuri, how he'd sputtered and blushed and set himself to spinning in the station's microgravity before Asami had relented, laughing.

It was only after she powered down the 'caster that she pulled herself, hand over hand through the station's microgravity, to the only solace she had left.

• • •

Back into the interface. Back below the Europan ice.

The ocean dim and silent, an endless shifting vista of murk beyond the circle of light where she swam, the patches of fluorescence from globefish on the hunt for prey lending such a depth to the scene that she could give herself over to the alien seascape fully, forgetting she was not truly there.

She swam for hours, watching tubeworms shrink away from her light, chasing schools of swallowfish as they darted through the periphery of her vision.

Occasionally she came across a fungal colony half-buried in the slush of the ocean floor, and the remote submersible's interface broke the illusion with a quiet chirrup as she pierced each colony as quickly as she could with the needle-like sample retriever and moved on.

She did not think about the recycled air she was breathing on Ling-Xian Station, about Hesheng and her mother back on Earth. She did not think of sandstorms and smog, of funeral fires and the fine white smoke that pours from chimneys after. She did not think about her mother and her stories of a sun that had been tame enough to gently warm the skin, of winds so calm they had set Anji's fabled bamboo forests creaking.

Most of all, she did not think about her daughters.

The plant life on the ocean floor swayed and bent, a miniature bamboo forest in a breeze made of dark blue water. Somewhere in these undersea reaches there was an answer. There had to be.

• • •

Time passed.

Minutes, hours in the forgetfulness of Europa before the chirrup of the interface returned her to the station. The days blending into one another in a bustle of resistance training and sweat, of kelp-and-soy brats and coffee tubes and tests and reports for Mission Control.

Yuri left, his replacement a Scottish woman named Fiona who made Asami as flustered as she'd made Yuri.

Life went on among the living, in other words, and below them the ice of Europa shifted endlessly, implacable, as old as life itself.

One day Yihan got a 'cast from her mother.

"Yihan," her mother's image said. "I know you hurt. I hurt, too; Every time Hesheng 'casts you I sit here and I watch. I'm happy you still have that wall scroll, but when will you forgive yourself for not being there at the end? When will you come back to us?"

There were lines under her mother's eyes, a tightness to the skin on her forehead Yihan did not remember seeing there before. How many months had it been since she came here? A year? More? What other things had she missed?

"I'm going to Anji," her mother continued. "I know it's nothing more than sand now. Hesheng does too, in spite of my stories. They studied the Great Desertification in school last month. But I want to see where my mother lived. Where *we* could have lived, if we hadn't been born too late.

"I've saved enough for Hesheng to stay here until she's old enough to leave." A pause, then, her mother's image looking off to one side. "I'm dying, Yihan," she said at last, her voice little more than a whisper. "It's not tuberculosis, but I'm dying all the same."

Yihan turned off the 'caster, hands trembling. From her spot on the wall, the girl on the scroll smiled with the innocence of youth, caught forever in the act of pulling up a pail of water from a river running through a faded bamboo forest.

• • •

That night, Yihan couldn't sleep. Strapped against the bed's hard surface, she tossed and turned for hours.

"Scopes," she whispered at last. "Surface."

She lay there staring at Conamara Chaos's bleak beauty until, at last, she drifted off.

Mercifully, she didn't remember her dreams.

• • •

The next morning, the 'caster had another message, this one from Hesheng.

"Mom," her daughter said, her eyes swollen, ugly in grief. "Grandma's going to Anji. She says the air there's so clean you can live in the open, listening to the bamboo creak in the wind. She says the birds fly by so close overhead you can touch them."

"She's lying, Mom. I know she is. She knows it herself." Hesheng ran the back of one arm across her eyes, sniffled. "I'm scared." Then, after a longer period of sniffling. "I'm sorry. I shouldn't have sent this."

And that was the end of the 'cast.

Yihan glanced up at the scroll her mother had given her, faded and peeling on Ling-Xian Station's too-white wall. White as a hospital's. She closed her eyes, imagined herself once more in the blue of the Europan ocean, then opened them again to take in Hesheng's picture, so perfect in its miniaturization.

What was she *doing*?

How had she decided that the way to make things

right was to travel out here? That her research would ever make up for her missing Xixi's final moments?

There were some things you could never make up for.

But there were also some you could. Fingers trembling, Yihan reached out and brushed the outline of Hesheng's cheek, then shut down the 'caster and launched herself into the commons to tell Asami and Fiona her decision. Someone else would have to hunt down exotic microbes in the icy Europan waters, because she was going home.

ABOUT THE AUTHOR

Stewart C Baker is an academic librarian, speculative fiction writer and poet, and the editor-in-chief of *sub-Q Magazine*. His fiction has appeared in *Nature*, *Galaxy's Edge*, and *Flash Fiction Online*, among other places. Stewart was born in England, has lived in South Carolina, Japan, and California (in that order), and currently resides in Oregon with his family—although if anyone asks, he'll usually say he's from the Internet.

TRIVALENT

Rivqa Rafael

Some days I think we should just let the viruses win. Viruses are simple. Viruses are easy. Sure, they might mutate in the blink of an eye and wipe out our species, but at least they don't have *feelings*. But no, survival instinct is stronger than misanthropy and so I kept working, trying to save people I can't stand from death and pain by mosquito-borne disease. Which is why I was sitting in a rickety chair, waiting for Larry to get to the lab meeting agenda item that said "publicly castigate Kay." Life choice regret levels: high.

At last he turned to me with a shit-eating grin. "Kay." Another lab manager might have spoken to me privately, but that wasn't Larry's style. He was all about "public accountability" and that kind of shit.

Resisting the urge to sit up straight in my chair, I replied, "Yes, Larry." Technically we were a co-op, doing science as best we could in a crumbling building with chipped glassware and homegrown agar. Government funding was a thing of the past, but there's always going to be a hierarchy, and being young and new meant I was low in the pecking order. All the hard work had happened when I was a kid, stranded in Cairns like so many people were, not understanding why we couldn't just get on a plane and go home. When I was old enough to join the co-op, they had food growing everywhere and a functional library (OK, so some of the books were getting tattered) and if you were tenacious and smart enough to learn the science as you went, you could get on a work roster and try to find a supervisor.

"We've discussed mutual respect and teamwork many times, Kay. And somehow it doesn't seem to sink in. I've lost track of the amount of times you were unacceptably rude to me or someone else."

"What about not talking to people when they've *finally* got a chance to use the cell culture hood? After other people have been hogging it for*ever*?" Under the hood, it's hard enough keeping two thoughts in your head: whatever you're actually doing, and keeping everything sterile. Put a lid down the wrong way and you've wasted half a day's work and a bottle of reagent. Do that enough times and you'll be assigned to the distillery to brew up more ethanol. (I know brew isn't the right word, shut up.) Point is, it's boring as batshit compared to actually growing viruses so you can try to mass murder them—the viruses, I mean. Which isn't even that exciting if you forget the endgame: no more dengue, chikungunya, zika, and everything else those bastard bloodsuckers carried around.

"That kind of attitude is exactly what I'm talking about. You can't just think about yourself, or even just your own subgroup."

Just because there were already dengue and malaria vaccines (even if they were kind of shit), and zika was *so* important because it involved babies and pregnant women. Yeah, I know, I'm all unnatural and not a proper woman because I don't want babies, but noooo thank you.

Chiku and "other" were left for the rest of us, but "other" was where I liked to play. It was less about vaccine development and more about studying the way the viruses mutated, trying to predict what might come next and kill us all while we worried too much about Guillain–Barré syndrome. It was the closest to basic science that I could get, seeing as basic science was a luxury and we were never, ever getting our jetpacks. "My subgroup gets the least time under the hood, and you had to pick right then to talk to me."

He hadn't even put on his lab coat. In the wet lab. And he stood *way* too close to me, hood or no hood. When I finally had a turn while the zika team seemed occupied with something super exciting. Fuck being polite under those circumstances, seriously. Especially when you should know better.

But no, he wasn't going to be drawn into any discussion about his shortcomings, and no one seemed willing to back me up. He sighed deeply and shook his head; if he was putting on the seriousness for a show he was actually doing a pretty good job of it. "What you need, Kay, is a secondment on another team. Learn to work with others, properly. We don't have the luxury of silos here. The epidemiology team needs another body for some fieldwork."

"You can't move me to epi." I couldn't keep the whinge out of my voice. "I've got no expertise. I don't even do my own stats. I have cultures in the incubator and they're really, really important!" Great, now I sounded like the zika team. Not what I was going for.

"The rest of your team can handle them, and epidemiology really needs you. It's not a punishment because it's busywork." He grinned around the faces at the lab meeting. "It's a punishment because you don't want to do it, Kay." Oh, he'd practised that one, I was sure of it.

The chairs squeaked in protest as people shifted in their seats, not meeting my eyes or Larry's.

I sank back into my own chair, defeated by the silence and by Larry. "So, what do you guys need?"

"We're heading out to the field to recruit for the next phase of the vaccine study." Fiona, who headed the zika epi group, folded her dimpled brown hands in her lap as she spoke, looking at the rest of her people rather than at me. I knew little about her, other than she was one of the last people to make it over from Thursday Island in time, before the whole Torres Strait went under. Oh, and she was a brilliant epidemiologist, but I'd kind of never paid attention. Nothing against that branch of science, I knew it was important, it just seemed so bloody boring. "Mike's farm was hit hard in the last cyclone. I gave him leave to go home to help his family rebuild."

"Recruitment?" My voice graduated from a whinge to a squeak. "Talking to people? Getting permission to stick them with needles? Oh, hell no." I was a virologist. Really, what I wanted to do was work on a project to squash every mosquito in the world, but apparently that wasn't a workable solution because whatever filled the niche in the ecosystem would spread the same diseases anyway, or similar ones. (Also, that's what you learn when you talk to scientists who can't take a joke.) So I settled on the next best thing and learned how to grow the viruses that they carried in cell cultures, in the hopes of developing vaccines that actually worked. Point was, I was not a people person and never would be.

"Without Mike, we really need someone." Fiona's voice was calm and level. "It's too much work for two, between the driving and keeping us safe and fed, apart from the actual work."

"Well, I can do some of that, anyway." Curse my

traitor of a mouth, but I was realising that she was pretty, and there was something mesmerising about her soft voice. "I'd hate to muck up your science."

"You did the phlebotomy course last year. Get a refresher this week and we'll fill you in on the rest."

"You read my file."

She didn't even blink, and as she replied I decided that I liked her. "Well, obviously. I wouldn't risk the study taking someone who couldn't pull their weight, no matter how hard Larry leaned."

Larry wore the expression of a man whose thunder had been well and truly stolen. He waved a hand at Fiona. "Work out the details on your own time. Next item?"

• • •

Finding myself unwilling to disappoint Fiona, I traded off a phlebotomy refresher for a session of cleaning and autoclaving the pathology lab's glassware. Fiona poked her head in as I practised attaching a tube to a child-sized needle. "Do the kids really sit still through this?"

"Sometimes," she said. "It helps if we can get a supply of local anaesthetic, numb the area first. Sometimes they freak out a bit, though."

"Awesome."

She patted my shoulder. "Don't worry, you can leave the tricky ones to us. Winnie—my nurse practitioner—is wonderful with kids."

"Bet you are, too," I found myself saying. Super smooth, that's me.

To her credit she didn't roll her eyes at me, just smiled politely and excused herself. That just made me like her more. Godfuckingdamnit.

• • •

We finished our preparations and packed up a few days later; I won't bore you with the details but of course we had to be self-sufficient and prepared for disaster, even though it wasn't cyclone season. All the supplies for the study, food, biodiesel, and camping gear made for a pretty packed Land Rover. Together with some of the other scientists, Larry waved us away as we left, his smug brain no doubt thinking of how nice it would be in the lab without me to tell him what a shithead he was.

Fiona had checked in with me regularly during the prep time, but I didn't meet Winnie until we were loading up the car. I guessed she was about my age, but it was hard to tell because she was super petite. She had a delicate look about her that made me think I'd snap her bones if I tried to hug her, so it was just as well she limited our meeting to a cool handshake. Whatever, she'd probably heard what a giant bitch I was. I'd sussed out that her team respected her practical skills, but not much more than that.

Winnie took the first shift driving while Fiona navigated and I sat crammed in the back seat with the gear. I had nothing in particular to do, so I practised keeping my mouth shut and sneaking glances at Fiona when I thought I could get away with it. She had a definite plan for where we were headed, although settlements rose and fell and moved quickly out here, so we had to stay flexible. It would be nice if people stayed put for follow-up in a year or more, but they weren't necessarily going to. Fiona and Winnie had to take so much into account with this kind of study, I was learning. I was as much in awe of their science as I was Fiona's unflappable demeanour. They chatted about their work and other things as we travelled, often in voices so soft I wasn't sure if they were even speaking English. When Fiona didn't need to navigate, she looked back at me occasionally but spent most of the time looking out the window or at Winnie. Probably making sure she wasn't getting too tired.

• • •

Our first stop was Mareeba, where there was a large, stable settlement with a dynamic Aboriginal Medical Service. A rusted sign with a faded smiling sun greeted us as we rolled in. "Low-hanging fruit first," Fiona said, and she wasn't wrong. Everyone seemed to know her, at least by sight. Winnie got a few nods as well, but mostly she hung behind Fiona. You'd have thought it would be a chance for Winnie and I to bond a bit, but you'd be wrong. Every time I tried to make small talk I got a one-word reply. If I was lucky. Small talk isn't exactly my strong point, but damn if it wasn't like talking to an agar plate.

After a while, I gave up and concentrated on setting up our clinic space in the AMS while Fiona organised the paperwork. Neither task took long: setting up for bloods and vaccinations was easy enough, and Fiona didn't exactly need to strain to convince the staff that the study was important and would benefit the community. The building was in better nick than most of the town—don't get me wrong, the town was doing OK but the AMS was squeaky clean, its stark white paint job eased by colourful dot paintings. Winnie had disappeared; annoyed as I was that she wasn't helping, it was kind of a relief. It was easier to stay quiet while I shifted boxes alone than it was with a wall of silence next to me.

Just as I finished unpacking the last carton, Winnie rounded the corner with a gaggle of kids, all following her like she was a tiny Pied Piper. They chattered excitedly while their parents trailed behind at a slower pace.

"School just finished," she said to Fiona. "Thought we may as well get started."

"The clinic will recruit for us, too. We'll probably be here most of tomorrow, at least."

Winnie nodded. "I promised these ones a game while we wait. And you-know-what after."

"Lollies!" The kids' screeching drilled into my skull. Fucking hell, how did such small people get so loud?

Fiona just smiled, head tilted a little as she watched. "Well, we're ready, and Kay can assist me. Who's first?" As they clamoured around her, she put a hand on my shoulder. "The eager ones shouldn't be difficult. This is a good place for you to start."

Swallowing the nervousness in my throat, I nodded. She flashed me a quick smile, her teeth bright white in a grin that lit up her whole face.

My job was easy enough. I set out the equipment for each participant while Fiona explained the trial to the parent and sorted out the consent forms. Then I gloved up, found a tiny vein, and slipped the tiny needle in for the blood test while Fiona distracted the kid by asking about school or whatever. As soon as I had the needle out, she grabbed their upper arm tightly and gave them the jab—the new dengue–malaria–zika shot for the trial group, or the old dengue–malaria vax for the controls. If I couldn't find a vein, Fiona did both, working as fast as she could to keep the trauma brief. Most of the kids were fine but some of them cried, each scream stabbing a knife into my brain.

The crowd never seemed to get any smaller, as word-of-mouth passed through the town and more people turned up. People wanted protection from the bugs, of course. But they were also thrilled to be in a study, even if they got the control shot. For some of the tiny kids, especially, it might have been their first encounter with structured science, and even I had to admit that was kind of cool. I wondered how many of them might show up in Cairns in a decade or so, begging for a job the way I had.

But the shine of that enthusiasm wore off as the evening dragged on. My head hurt and I was hungry. And still people kept coming. At eight o'clock, Winnie handed out tokens for the last ten participants and sent everyone else home, promising the kids that the lollies would still be there tomorrow. When one of the Aunties showed up with a basket of hot food, I nearly hugged her. But I wasn't the hugging type, and hugging an Aboriginal Elder I didn't know definitely wasn't my style. We went to sleep soon after, aware that we'd be doing the same thing the next day.

• • •

And so we were, until the last kid and woman of childbearing age was stabbed and jabbed. The second day was much like the first, except that as the day wore on there were more difficult kids, just like Fiona had predicted. Some of them clung to their parents like limpets; more than one wouldn't let me near and screamed for Winnie, who entered smug mode whenever she had to snap on her gloves for one of those.

"Why doesn't she just do all the bloods then,

instead of playing with the kids?" I muttered to myself.

Unfortunately for me, Fiona heard. "Because then you'd have to keep the kids out there happy," she said, one eyebrow arched. "Happy kids out there makes our job in here easier. It's real work, you know. Unless you'd rather do it."

You'll be glad to hear I kept my mouth shut for the rest of the day, even after we left Mareeba and set up camp that evening. Impressive effort on my part, I know.

That night I lay awake for what felt like hours, trying my best to will away the throbbing in my head. My ears were still popping from the undulating road through the Tableland, too. After a while I heard one tent unzip and rezip, then the other. Soon there were soft voices talking, laughing, and eventually moaning. Every muscle in my body clenched in a futile attempt to protect myself against the simultaneous arousal and disappointment. Of course Fiona and Winnie were together, keeping it on the down-low to avoid scrutiny (or worse) from Larry. Of course no one wanted to cuddle me—or do anything else with me—in a tent in the middle of nowhere. I wondered if Mike felt the same way when he was on these field trips, but no, he had a partner and a little baby. It was 2 a.m. in Far North Queensland and I'd never felt more alone.

Of course, it was about to get worse.

• • •

The next day, it took me an extra coffee to feel awake enough to drive. I tried a new technique for keeping my mouth shut—clenching my teeth together tightly enough to hurt. It worked, apart from a couple of brow-furrowed glances from Fiona. Winnie loitered at the campsite until Fiona climbed into the passenger seat behind me. Did I smell bad enough that neither of them wanted to sit next to me? It was worse than primary school, being one of the interstate strays that no one wanted or cared about. Fiona slammed her door shut with uncharacteristic vigour. Blinking, I shrugged and turned the ignition. No clue what that was about, and I didn't think I wanted to know. It's bad enough to think that nobody likes you, but being sure would be worse.

Uncomfortable silence hung in the Land Rover as we hurtled down what used to be a highway. The government used to maintain the roads, but that was left to the locals now. If there were any. More than once, I had to slow down to circumvent a pothole so deep that even the Land Rover wouldn't cope. And once I swerved around a pack of wild boar, but I couldn't imagine the government doing much about those. Feral species were truly here to stay.

We drove for hours without seeing another vehicle, let alone a settlement. I was wondering how close to Cape York we'd get when I saw it: just a shimmer in a valley up ahead. "Is that a township?" I asked.

"I don't see anything," Winnie said.

Leaning forward in her seat, Fiona frowned a little. "I've got no record of a community here. Slow down, would you?"

We crept closer, looking for the obvious hallmarks of anything that might be dangerous; there were cults out here, and straight-up gun nuts. A wire fence encircled the settlement, but it wasn't barbed or particularly high. Clusters of small wooden huts seemed to have been placed at random inside, and patches of sugar cane and fruit tree saplings filled the spaces between. You could almost smell the patchouli from here. "Looks like harmless hippies to me," I said.

"I don't like it," Winnie said. "They weren't here last time we came through. We should come back with a bigger team."

Fiona was quiet for a few moments before she spoke. I could have sworn she was counting to ten. "If they really are hippies they're not likely to sign up."

"But you never know, do you?" I tried my best to be chirpy. Fake optimism is better than none, right? "Don't you want to get home quicker?"

The silence was deafening that time, despite the rattle of the engine. Fiona's expression didn't change but her eyes slid away from me.

Finally, Winnie spoke, tone gentle as though she were speaking to a child. "That was rude."

"What the fuck?" I'd stepped in it, I knew that, but

I had no idea how.

She looked at Fiona pointedly. "Some people *can't* go home."

I killed the engine; we'd idled long enough. "If you're going to be overly literal about it, neither can I. Unless you have enough biodiesel to get me down the coast. Then all I'd have to do is swim across Bass Strait, easy. Seriously, what's your problem?" I wasn't touchy about the word home, and at least mine was still there (as far as we knew), but it hurt all the same.

"That's enough!" Fiona said, before Winnie—who, I'll give her credit, was looking a bit chagrined—could reply. Fiona's hands were balled into tight fists on her lap. "We'll check out this settlement. If only to get *back to Cairns* sooner."

Winnie flounced back in her seat and I started the engine again. It should have felt like a victory, but I had a feeling that nobody had won that round.

• • •

After parking the Land Rover at the correct distance, we wordlessly followed the protocol for approaching a strange settlement. Weapons remained in the vehicle, along with all our supplies. Fiona carried her tablet over her head, its screen blank white to show we meant no harm. My guts churned and my head was stormy, but even so it was a bit of a surprise when the gates swung open of their own accord. Pretty high-tech for your garden-variety hippies.

Right after we'd stepped inside, Fiona said, "Shit, the back-to-base message."

I unlocked my own datapad. It wasn't picking up any sort of signal, not even the local radio network. "Fuck."

The gate slammed shut behind us and my heart dropped into the pit that was already festering in my stomach.

• • •

They made us wait. Classic intimidation. After a while, Winnie started complaining, but she shut up when Fiona elbowed her. Good. At least I didn't have to deal with it. I got over being scared and moved on to angry, my fists clenched by my sides and my heart thundering. Fight or flight, flight or fight. Fleeing would be the best move, of course, but goddamn if I didn't want the fight.

There was another gate a few metres ahead, so we were trapped between the two. At long last, a man appeared on the other side of the inner gate. He wore the crumpled hemp you'd expect, and his hair had been shaved so recently it was impossible to tell what colour it was. His face and forearms were tanned dark, but his skin was noticeably paler around the cuffs and neckline of his T-shirt. "Place your hands where we can see them and state your purpose."

We'd ended up standing back to back, forming a little triangle. That pit in my stomach gnawed; we were three women, outnumbered and vulnerable. By unspoken agreement, Fiona spoke for us. "We're from the university in Cairns and we're vaccine researchers."

"Scientists, here to experiment on us? Isn't that … interesting."

"If your community doesn't want to participate, we'll move on," Fiona said hurriedly.

"Yes, you will. But we'll need to scan you before you can leave."

"Scan us? For what?" Winnie's voice was so soft, I could hardly hear it.

"GMOs, pesticides, any devices that emit a signal."

"How are you going to—" Fiona asked, at the same time as I said, "Why, if you're going to let us go?"

He crossed his arms over his chest. "Who knows what you've already released without us knowing it? Something airborne, maybe, or tiny robots?"

"Nanobots are just slightly outside our funding capabilities these days," I snapped.

"So you say."

Fiona mirrored his position. "Yes we do. And as we've done nothing of the sort, you're more than welcome to scan us. We'd like to be on our way as soon as possible."

Yellow-stained teeth appeared as his mouth curved into an unkind smile. "I'll need the keys to your vehicle."

Hands shaking, Fiona held the key out. "Please be careful with our supplies … they're important to many people, if not you."

Sneering, he carelessly dropped the key into a colourful pocket. "So you say."

Fight took over me then. My face felt like a furnace with ears for exhaust pipes. I grabbed his arm, tight as I could. "Hey, most people around here would rather avoid dengue, even if you're happy to have it 'cause it's *natural*, you mung bean."

Shaking off my hand easily, his expression hardly changed apart from his blue eyes burning. "What's that? You'd like to be locked up while we search your things and scan your bodies?"

"No!" Fiona pulled me back by my shoulders. "She doesn't mean anything by it, she's just upset. Isn't that right, Kay?"

He ignored her and pulled out a walkie-talkie, requesting backup. For a second, I forgot how angry I was; I was too dumbfounded by the hypocrisy.

Fiona let go of my shoulders and gave me a look that shrank me down to a five-year-old. "Great work, Kay. Really well done." Winnie just stood there, trembling. No doubt I'd cop her reaction later.

Tilting my chin up defiantly, I put on my best brave face. "They won't do anything to us, I'm sure." Fiona's expression didn't change. "I'll keep my mouth shut, I swear."

"I'll believe that when I see it," she said.

"I will!" I said. "And you'll fix it, you're good at the diplomacy thing. I ... I'm sorry."

And that was all I had time to say, before another two dudes showed up and marched Fiona and Winnie in one direction, while Bald Mung Bean took me in another.

Well, fuck.

• • •

Over my shoulder, I could see them taking Fiona and Winnie into a nearby building. Apparently, I had a longer walk, along a gravel path lined with sugar cane (organic, I assumed). Up close, I could see how hastily the buildings had been constructed; the wood still looked pretty new and splintery, and there were gaps between the planks that would let mosquitoes in. I wondered if they used bed nets here, with or without insect repellent. That aside, this place would be screwed if a cyclone hit. If there were proper cellars, I'd eat my datapad.

Taking deep breaths, I tried my best to take in my surroundings, to stay calm. To not think about the possibility that I was about to be raped and/or murdered. I could take this guy if I had to. If he didn't have a gun, which he probably did. Would he hesitate to use it, out here where no one apart from his own people would ever know?

I had to look around, see if I could see anything

useful, and definitely not think about the dodgy truck driver who'd tried to convince Mum that he could drive us back down to Melbourne, that he knew a guy who crossed the strait all the *time*, luv. How he leered at me more than her. This guy wasn't like that. Oh, how I hoped I wasn't just telling myself that.

It was a gorgeous day: balmy, but it was still pretty early and safe from UV. And there were plenty of people around; they hadn't sounded an alarm and must have known we were harmless. But there were no kids playing outside, like you'd imagine hippie kids doing. Just adults, mostly men, but a few women, and not dressed like cult slaves either. At a guess, not more than thirty people lived here. I stored that bit of information to think about later and walked along obediently. Sure, I could have made a run for it, but with Fiona and Winnie (and the Land Rover keys) elsewhere, there wasn't much point. There weren't going to be any heroics from me; Fiona would smooth things over and we'd be on our way, hopefully sooner rather than later. It'll be fine, I repeated to myself as we walked. I'd only run if I absolutely had to. After kicking Bald Mung Bean in the nuts. Only if I had to.

We stopped at a rather large building on the very edge of the settlement. Bald Mung Bean grinned. "There's a lovely broom closet for you to ... wait in," he said. As if on cue, a wailing noise started up from inside the building, soon joined by others, each more aggravating than the last. I'd found the kids. He couldn't have devised a worse form of torture if he'd known me. Every muscle in my body stiffened and he had to half-drag me in. Clamping my jaw shut, I willed myself not to beg as he shoved me into a cupboard that hardly had room for me among all the other crap.

"We'll have a chat to your friends and scan them, and we'll be back for you soon. Won't be long!"

Pulling my lips in behind my teeth to keep myself quiet, I ignored the false cheeriness. He shut the door and turned the key, and I was alone in the dark. With screaming all around me.

• • •

It was hard to keep a sense of time. Bald Mung Bean had confiscated my datapad so I had no clock and no light source. At least it wasn't pitch black; a bit of light shone in from the cracks in the door frame, and my eyes gradually adjusted to the darkness. Not that there was anything much to see. The kids didn't scream all the time, but when they did I curled up and jammed my fingers in my ears as tight as I could.

When they were quiet, I listened for the whine of mosquitoes and slapped them dead as they landed. It was the least I could do, given that we weren't going to be vaccinating these kids. Not that I owed the little shits any favours, but even I knew that they weren't doing it on purpose. No, I saved all my anger for Bald Mung Bean and his mates, who were doing this to me to build up their egos and justify their bullshit philosophy. Fiona would sort him out and then I'd be out of this cupboard that was really a bit too much like the storage crates in the back of a truck—I pushed that thought away and listened out for the kids, who were pretty quiet right then.

There were no sounds of happy playing either, though. Was it nap time? Did kids nap in the morning? Was it even still morning? I had no idea but these kids sounded nothing like the (mostly) happy bunch at Mareeba or the kids I saw in Cairns (from a distance, admittedly). I didn't know enough about kids to work this out. Winnie or Fiona could have, but I wasn't them. So I did the only thing I could think of. Banging as hard as I could on the door, I yelled, "I need to pee! Please! Somebody!" Nothing. "I guess I'll have to pee on the floor then."

Footsteps, and an anxious woman's voice outside. "Promise you'll go back in when you're done or Derek will kill me."

"I won't cause any trouble. I swear."

The lock clicked open and a tall, pale woman opened the door. Her eyes had a vacant look about them, and she seemed to be several months pregnant. "Good, because we have enough."

All *right* then. She pointed to the left and I started walking, looking around as best I could without being too obvious and craning my neck. She walked along behind me, breathing loudly, as though it was an effort. I had almost despaired of seeing anything when she told me to turn a corner. "It's to the left," she said, but to the right I could see the answer to the puzzle.

Through the doorway was a room filled with about five cots, each with a baby or small child in it. These days, anyone can spot microcephaly a mile off. The kids here all had it, to some degree or another. The distended heads, the scrawny, out-of-proportion limbs. Vacant stares and drool and the smell of shit and vinegar. I wasn't in the daycare; I was in the hospital.

Jaw hanging loose, I stood as though rooted in place. "So many ..."

"Please, you need to move," she hissed urgently.

"Right." Forcing my head around, I turned and went into the bathroom, and used it (I really had needed to).

She was waiting for me outside. For a moment, we just stared at each other. "That door's supposed to be closed," she said.

So was my mouth, but some promises were meant to be broken. "Yeah I'll bet. *Derek* wouldn't want anyone seeing what you lot have swept under the rug. This is fucking child abuse, you know. There are people who can help, in Cairns. Speechies and OTs." I spared a thought for those speech and occupational therapists. Overworked but so compassionate ... more than I ever could be. "They teach parents a lot, you might not even need to stay there." I looked pointedly at her belly. "But why risk the WiFi signals for that, hey?"

She burst into tears. "There's nothing left in Cairns, the cyclones got everything."

"The beachfront hotels, mostly. The uni's still there, and we built a hospital on the campus. And we've rebuilt a lot. What rock have you been living under?"

"You're ... you're rude." She wiped at her eyes with her sleeve.

The tears quenched my first response, to say something even nastier. "I ... I am. I'm sorry. This must be difficult."

She nodded. "I have to take you back now."

When she opened the door and motioned me in, there was nothing left to lose. "Is this what you want for your baby? Nearly everyone's had zika these days, and I can't smell any insect repellent. The herbal shit does nothing."

She shut the door and locked it. Started sobbing as she walked away. What a waste that it was me here and not Fiona, who could have actually made a difference. I could only hope she wouldn't risk telling Derek, in case she got herself into trouble. Fuck, this place was weird. It didn't *look* culty, but it had the feel of it, and it galled me that I couldn't do anything about it. I sat back on my heels and listened for mosquitoes again.

• • •

At least twenty minutes later, there was a knock on the door. "Uh … come in?" I scrambled to my feet.

The door swung open to reveal a group of five women, including the one from before. "I'm Kate," she said, "and we want the vaccine. I haven't had zika, I'm sure of it. I've been careful."

"We want to know exactly what's in Cairns for our babies," another said.

Standing there in shock for a few moments was probably a good thing, because I had time to remind myself to be polite. "I, um … what about Derek?"

"We'll talk to him."

"I'm electrosensitive," Kate said, and I used all my strength to stop myself from scoffing. "But I'll take the headaches if it'll help my baby. Is … is there ultrasound at the hospital?"

I opened my mouth and closed it a few times. "Look, I'm a virologist, I work at the university. I'm not a clinician and I can't give you specific details or anything, but I know that they exist, and if we can radio in, you can ask them. But, like, you do know how jammers work, right? They're emitting a *radio* signal, and you're using walkie-talkies and scanners here … but you're not—" I bit my tongue as Kate crossed her arms over her belly. "I'll shut up. What do you want me to do?"

"Just tell us what you do know, and what you're

doing here. Then we'll put you back in and speak to Derek."

• • •

So I did, and they did. Apparently most of the kids here had parents who couldn't deal, and one mother had died in childbirth. There were other kids around, with and without birth defects. Not knowing how long Derek was planning to leave me in there for, we made it quick. If I thought I was tense before, the wait while they went to confront him was an agony of guts churning and head aching. I still killed mosquitoes, aided by the wind-up torch Kate had left with me, but it wasn't my best effort.

At long last, though, the door swung open once more, and Kate was there alone. "He said I may as well get you and bring you to the others." She was silent and calm during the walk, and I followed suit. Or tried to, anyway.

As well as Fiona, Winnie, and Derek, a handful of men and at least ten women were gathered in the office Kate led me to. Word must have spread, and they spoke to each other in low voices. Fiona and Winnie seemed worn and baffled. I just looked at them, too nervous to even wave. Fiona gave a tiny smile. Winnie looked away.

The talking didn't stop when Derek cleared his throat; he had to try a second time. "Apparently," he said, venom dripping, "the values of our community aren't very important to some people here, who'd rather pump chemicals through their bodies and expose themselves to radiation than have natural remedies—"

One of the men interrupted. "When was the last time you changed nappies in the hospital, Derek?"

"One of those kids is *yours*," Kate said. Well, fuck me dead, no one had mentioned that before. "We deserve to make this decision for ourselves, not to sit around while you lock people who can help us in a broom closet."

Derek threw his hands up. "If you don't want what I'm offering, fine. Leave."

The room buzzed with conversation. I kept myself quiet, quiet, quiet.

"I'd like my keys back now, please," Fiona said. Her voice was so soft and yet it cut through all the talk, which died off almost immediately. Derek made a weird sort of incoherent screaming noise and handed them over. Fiona curled her fingers around them tightly and spoke a little louder. "We'll be outside at our vehicle for the next hour for anyone who wants our help, or just wants to ask questions. We require consent forms before we give any vaccinations." She glared lasers at Derek, then walked out the door without a backwards glance.

• • •

We moved the Land Rover a little further away

from the settlement, just far enough to get a signal again. No one had followed us out after the gates swung open; they might have all had a change of heart, but I was pretty confident that they were just giving us some space. Nice of them. Fiona opened the pop-up tent and I put out some folding chairs underneath it. As Fiona set down a citronella coil, Winnie collapsed onto the ground, crying with great hiccupy sobs. Of course, she'd waited until the tent's tarp was conveniently beneath her. Fiona dropped the matches and ran over to wrap an arm around Winnie, stroking her hair with the other hand.

I lit the mozzie coil and walked around to the other side of the Land Rover, resting my elbows on the bonnet and my head in my hands. Winnie would definitely want space from me, and so would Fiona. As much as that stung, I needed it, too. Not to cry, just to breathe the fresh, unimpeded air. So it was a bit of a shock to feel a hand on my shoulder.

"You did good," Fiona said.

"I did shit, but thanks." My voice came out muffled by my hands, but I wasn't ready to look into her gorgeous eyes just yet. "Winnie okay?"

"She's fine. Just shock." Her hand was still on my shoulder, the pressure warm and gentle.

I stiffened, unsure of whether I could handle the contact even if she meant nothing by it. Other than not completely hating my guts, anyway. "It wasn't fun.

I'm sorry."

She moved her hand away and leaned in to peek through my curtain of hair. "I mean, your methods might not be ideal. But I think you got us more participants than we would have otherwise."

And by the crowd of people pouring out of the gate, it looked like she was right.

Winnie had stopped crying and gave us—*me!*—a very tiny smile. Fiona nodded at each of us in turn. Taking a breath, I let myself smile too.

ABOUT THE AUTHOR

Rivqa Rafael writes speculative fiction about queer women, Jewish women, cyborg futures, and hope in dystopias. Her short stories have been published in *GlitterShip*, *Escape Pod*, Crossed Genres' *Resist Fascism*, and elsewhere, and she recently co-edited award-winning feminist robot anthology *Mother of Invention*. She can be found online at rivqa.net or on Twitter as @enoughsnark.

AT CLIMATE COURT

Jeff Hecht

Two crisply uniformed young guards pushed Jill's grandfather into the courtroom in a wheelchair. It hurt her to see him so frail. She remembered him standing tall, proud, and vigourous at her side when she married Susannah.

When Jill was growing up, her grandfather had headed a billion-dollar petroleum company. He would call her on video as he travelled around the world. "Our business is energy," he would tell her. "We make the world go round." Four years after the wedding, his first stroke left his speech slurred, but his mind was intact and he soon was walking again. The second stroke hit him harder, and he had still been in recovery when the climate police came for him.

The family had been stunned. The climate police already had forced the company into liquidation, but no one had thought they would arrest him.

Fortunately, Jill's grandfather had provided well. The family could afford the best hospitals for his treatment and the best lawyers for his defense. But the climate court would not grant him bail. Now that the trial had come, Jill had used almost a year of her carbon allowance to fly to the Netherlands to be with him in jail and at the trial. It was the least she could do after he had stood for her at the wedding after her parents had refused. She remembered him smiling as he told Susannah's parents, "You're family now," welcome without regard to race, religion, or politics.

The day before the trial began, Jill spent thirty minutes with her grandfather in jail, but he said little. Afterwards, his lead lawyer told Jill they had a solid defense. Now her grandfather slumped in the prison wheelchair, his good arm struggling to push his thin white hair back into place as one guard pushed the wheelchair into a clear plastic box, where her grandfather sat beside his lawyer facing the judge.

The judge called on the two lead prosecutors, who sat at a table of real wood. Jill's mobile told her that Nasiruddin was the name of the thin dark man who spoke for victims of the great Bangladesh supercyclone and their families. Jill shivered when the bent grey-haired woman who followed said that she had lost her name when she lost her homeland of Tuvalu to the rising sea.

When they had finished, her grandfather's lead lawyer rose. "Mr. Friedman has been disabled by a severe stroke," she said. "I am fully informed of his affairs and he and his family have authorized me to speak for him."

The judged asked her grandfather to confirm the lawyer's statement. He nodded wordlessly, his body slumped in his chair. His back was to Jill, but she was sure he knew she was there.

"Mr. Friedman, you are charged with committing environmental crimes leading to the loss of lives and homelands," the judge began. "As chief executive of WDMX Petroleum, you certified as accurate a research report that claimed carbon-dioxide emissions from petroleum-based fuels had caused no more than 0.1 degree of global warming since 1950. Last year this court ruled that report was a deliberate fraud and part of a conspiracy orchestrated by fossil fuel companies and some government officials to hide the imminent impact of human activity on global climate. This court also ruled that fraud was responsible for the loss of the homeland of Tuvalu and of over 150,000 lives in Bangladesh. Under the Global Environmental Crime treaty, you are subject to a term of life imprisonment for each offense. How do you plead?"

The lead defense counsel looked at the judge. "Under the laws of the United States, a chief executive officer must act as a fiduciary for the benefit of corporate stockholders," she said. "We will show that duty absolves our client of guilt for environmental crimes because admitting that the company's products made a major contribution to climate change would have led to sales restrictions that would have reduced or eliminated company profits, and thereby violated his fiduciary responsibility by harming stockholders. He had no choice but to obey those strictures given the requirements of his role."

The judge stared poker-faced at the lawyer for what seemed like a long time before responding. "Are you saying that your client is innocent because he was only following orders ?"

The lawyer looked pleased with the judge's interpretation. "Yes, your honour."

"Do you concur, Mr. Friedman?" the judge asked.

Jill's grandfather coughed as he looked up. "NO!" he said in a hoarse and slurred but firm voice. Jill, the prosecutors, the lawyers, and the courtroom turned as he struggled with his words. "I was a fool and a coward. I didn't want it to be true, so I denied it and pretended it would go away." Jill heard him wheeze. "I am guilty. We are all guilty. Take me away!"

His head slumped, and in the moment of silence that followed, Jill heard him say, "I'm sorry, Jill." She saw him start to cry before she closed her eyes to contain her own tears. She could not face having to watch the guards wheel him back to jail.

ABOUT THE AUTHOR

Jeff Hecht is a freelance science and technology writer based in the Boston area who covers topics from climate and evolution to lasers and dinosaurs for magazines including *New Scientist, Nature, IEEE Spectrum, Sky & Telescope,* and *Laser Focus World.* He also writes short science fiction which has been published in *Nature Futures, Daily Science Fiction, Analog, Interzone, Asimov's,* and other magazines and anthologies. His latest book is *Lasers, Death Rays, and the Long, Strange Quest for the Ultimate Weapon,* published this year by Prometheus Books.

GAC ATG ATT ACA

Melanie Harding-Shaw

Erika liked to think of herself as a gene artist. That was how she kept the despair at bay in the claustrophobic bunker deep under the ground. She had never stood on the earth's surface; neither had her mother, grandmother, or many generations before them.

Instead, she worked to keep the gene pool viable in the small population here. She carefully designed each new baby and recorded their genome in the computer for future geneticists to reference. In her lifetime she had added two generations to the records. Current estimates were that short trips to the surface may finally be possible in three years. She might live that long—just.

She'd discovered the code in the notebooks of her predecessor when she first started working. She had relished the challenge of sequencing a genetically viable child that also contained a message for future generations. Once she knew what to look for it was time-consuming, but not complicated, to find the line in each person's DNA that contained the message. The texts were all short—only a single sentence per person. It had taken her a year to realise that she could follow the messages down generations of a family to create a longer work. A poem. Art.

Some families' genes contained descriptions of the world, told through the words of changing gene artists who had all felt the same despair:

The sky is just a story now.
Walls close in around us.
Hope is for the future.
We exist always in today.

Sometimes the messages were more personal and stood alone. There wasn't space for everyone who wanted a child to have one:

I am the treasured culmination of a generation of longing.

Erika had thought about telling her replacement the secret of the code, but she hadn't wanted to deny him the excitement of the discovery in their unchanging world. Now she spent her twilight years looking back through the records, assembling and reassembling their poems. She looked right back to the first postapocalyptic generations.

Toxicity levels on the surface were one year from dropping to safe levels when she came across the records of an early family line that had not continued. The notes said they had sacrificed their own procreation rights so another couple could have a child. Their poetry had been lost to future gene artists. There were only two generations recorded:

We are not alone in the world, I will find the others. Latitude -41.28664, Longitude 174.77557

Erika stared at the screen and started to cry. She had never dared to believe that another outpost of humanity might exist. Every child of the bunker was raised with stories of the people who had tried to leave and died from exposure to the harsh and toxic surface world. It didn't stop a handful trying every generation and breaking the hearts of those left behind. She could understand why someone would hide this information.

She looked up the geneticist who had left the coordinates all those generations ago and then she looked up the code of their only child. It contained the shortest message she'd ever found. So short she almost overlooked it—*GAC ATG ATT ACA*: Hope.

ABOUT THE AUTHOR

Melanie Harding-Shaw is a speculative fiction writer, policy geek, and mother-of-three from Wellington, New Zealand. Her work has appeared in publications like *Daily Science Fiction* and *The Arcanist*, and she was a finalist for Best Short Story in the 2019 Sir Julius Vogel Awards. You can find her at www.melaniehardingshaw.com.

THE LAST STAND

Christoph Weber

A thirty-foot wave of flame roars toward us over the grassy plain. We stand our ground. We were soldiers once.

Behind us loom the titans of California Redwood Emergency Preserve. *Sequoia sempervirens.* The world's tallest trees. Their foliage trembles in the wind like frightened fingers. Our assignment is to keep them alive. In years past, that wasn't hard: coast redwoods have insulating bark over a foot thick, making them highly resistant to typical wildfires.

Typical is not a word I'd use today.

I lean around the heat shield of our Humvee's turret toward my second gunner, kneeling in the truck's bed. "You ready, Em?"

She slaps her machine gun playfully, but her eyes are focused. She grew up here on the Redwood Coast. So did I. When our forces wrote off California, when they left to salvage what they could in Oregon and Washington, we stayed behind. For us, this is personal.

I shout at our driver. "Spud, punch it!"

Dust billows from our Humvee's tires as it speeds along our forested bank. The river is all that stands between our redwoods and the approaching grass fire. The fuel break the water provides is not enough.

But it's about to get wider.

Em and I pull our triggers simultaneously. Incendiary rounds stream from our gun barrels and over the river, the red tracers like lasers through fog. They burrow into the far bank's crisp grass tinder and a thousand fires leap to life. For a moment it's like a spring from my youth, a phantom of the golden poppy fields that once graced our state. The gold blooms coalesce into a snake of flame that sidewinds to meet the charging orange wave.

There's a saying, that you can't fight fire with fire. It's nonsense. Dumping water on today's infernos is like pissing on a house fire. These days fire is the *only* way to fight fire. And that's what we're doing: lighting a backburn to clear out all the grass in the main fire's path, to starve it to death.

When you work with fire you start to see it as a living creature. Just a hungry animal with a life cycle not unlike ours. Fires are born, they eat, they grow, they die. They even breathe like us—inhaling oxygen, exhaling carbon dioxide. And a fire running as fast as this one can suck serious wind, gasping in a constant breath that pulls the ground-level air inward to replace its convective exhalation.

And that's its weakness. That inflow wind pulls our backburn *toward* the oncoming wave, consuming all the fuel between them. When they meet, both fires will starve, wither, and die.

"It's lagging!" Em shouts.

She's right. Unless we speed up our backburn, the main fire will crash over it, hop the river, and devour the redwoods. Us, too, if we get pinched.

Far out in the grass, I spot a patch of fallen trees not fully consumed in previous fires. Once, this was all redwood forest. It took decades of drought for fire to finally gain a foothold here, but it arrived hungry: carbon that had taken the ancient forests millennia to capture was released back to the atmosphere in just a few seasons, initiating a feedback cycle that resulted in more warming, more lightning, more fires, and more overtime hours than I ever wanted.

But those downed trees on the plain didn't fully burn in the last fire, and if I can get them to ignite again they'll heat things up, help our backburn move faster. "Em, PIG!"

She hands me the propelled incendiary grenade launcher. I shoulder the weapon, pull the trigger. The PIG hisses like an angry cat as it speeds toward the fallen trees, exploding in a flash of white that drives back the shadow of overhead smoke. Flames scurry from the woodpile toward the main front, encouraging our trailing backburn to charge faster.

Fueled by the roiling air, a tornado of flame leaps from the oncoming front like an upright, angry serpent. It tears toward us through the grass, through our backburn, and into the charred area just across the river. The lower half of the whirl flickers from orange to black. I grin. Starved of fuel, it's coughing, choking on the ash.

Then, in the hyperoxygenated, superheated vortex, the ash re-ignites. The revitalized serpent storms to the river's edge, spits embers over the water. Firebrands drift down into the redwoods like an infernal snow. Em's upturned, wide eyes glow with fear and firelight.

"Spud, heavy foot!" I flip my radio to air-to-ground two as our Humvee accelerates. "Firebird, this is Dragonslayer One, requesting *immediate* extraction. Over."

As Spud tears along the riverbank, I look to the redwoods, to those titans who, having survived millennia of fire, now witness their age come to an end. Flames lick at their trunks like lustful tongues, then begin to climb the once-moist protective bark, desiccated after years of record heat and drought. I think of my childhood, of climbing that same bark, my fingers finding holds deep in their furrowed armour. Now, the titans writhe and groan in the roiling wind. Orange ascends to their foliage and the canopy explodes in a dance of flames, drunk on destruction as they leap from tree to tree.

Spud skids our truck under the hovering Chinook. Em and I connect the chopper's hanging cables to our Humvee's slings and then we're airborne, swinging in the turbulence. I tell myself the world will go on, and it will. But my children will not know these trees as I did, and already that grieves me. With one hand on the truck's frame, I lean over and squeeze Em's shoulder. When she looks back, her welling eyes mirror the infernal dance below.

"I'm sorry," I mouth over the throb of rotors, over the screams of immolating trees.

She turns away. There's nothing left to say.

All we can do is watch four-hundred-foot flames devour the last stand of redwoods.

ABOUT THE AUTHOR

A former firefighter with two interagency hotshot crews, Christoph Weber is now a certified arborist, board member at the University of Nevada Arboretum, and guerrilla tree planter. His short fiction has appeared in *Nature*, *Deep Magic*, and VICE's *Terraform*, was included on *Tangent Online*'s Recommended Reading List, and won the Writers of the Future Award. For more of Christoph's work, and to stay apprised of his debut novel, *Hangman*, stop by christophweber.com.

Readers of the "Last Stand" have donated over $1,000 to help those displaced by California wildfires. To join in their generosity, please visit the California Fire Foundation.

AN OASIS OF AMENDS

Floris M. Kleijne

You should have seen this, Rowan.

From the observation platform on the converted oil rig, I watch the giant conveyor lift the chunks out of the Atlantic Ocean, see them climb to the coastal plain of Mauritania, see the freeway width of the belt disappear over the horizon, and feel like a LEGO figurine in a life-sized industrial zone.

The solid wall of noise makes me sweat as much as the heat does. The shouting, the mechanical roar of the conveyor, the screaming crunch of the ice, and the shattering splashes of the chunks crashing back into the ocean make it hard to think. So I don't think, but let the memory of you pervade me, a bittersweet sensation I love and dread.

· · ·

While I was still trying to fight the greenhouse effect, lobbying for emission agreements, investing billions in sustainable energy, strengthening sea walls around the globe, you were way ahead of me. I called you a pessimist when you said global warming was a given, the inevitable result of humanity's carelessness. You told me nothing we could do to mitigate our mistakes would have measurable effects on any useful time scale. You argued that it was too late to fight causes, that all our influence and wealth were better spent dealing with the consequences. I called you fatalistic, mocked you for a harbinger of doom.

In the end, you relented, chose our marriage over your beliefs. This keeps me awake at night, that you gave in, relinquished your conviction to support my follies instead. Is that what love does to us?

I should have listened to you.

• • •

Another iceberg drifts stately into the bay, a surreal sight against a background of blistering Sahel coast. A trio of power pushers and its own embedded engines propel it into the maws of the Nutcracker. You would have loved that name. The enormous steel jaws rise from the waves and squeeze together, seeming to stop dozens of metres from the tip of the iceberg. Under water, the automatic drills deliver their charges, and the berg shudders with muffled explosions, the jaws recommencing their unrelenting squeeze until the ice shatters into house- and car-sized chunks.

As the Nutcracker opens, the sweeper ships move in, herding the chunks deeper into the bay. For all its violence and chaos, the operation runs smoothly, and in fifteen minutes, the first chunks rise from the ocean to be conveyed inland.

The explosions, the waves, the rumbling of the conveyor travel through the rig until my chest vibrates. Sweating, I climb the stairs to the ancient waiting Chinook, its twin rotors attempting to overwhelm the symphony of shudders.

This is how the dyke shook before it collapsed.

. . .

We were there at the breach when the Netherlands were lost. An apocalyptic landscape of roiling black clouds darkened the sky over the North Sea. Merciless wind tore at the marram grass, whipped the beach sand to abrasive frenzy. Thunderous waves took giant bites out of the Dutch dunes even as the Zeeland Delta Works succumbed to the onslaught. The evacuation of the country, which I had fought to postpone because the sea wall would damn well hold, wasn't even halfway complete.

Was it guilt that kept me hauling sand bags? Was it love that kept you by my side? At least I know what it was when the dyke crumbled, and you were swept away while I was dragged to safety, screaming your name until my throat bled.

That was punishment.

. . .

I'm making amends now, Rowan. Don't mourn what's already lost, you told me. Deal with what's left.

You're gone, my love, but I'm still here.

"They're *going* to melt," you said, shrugging. "Both of them, north and south. There is no way you can reverse that process now."

"But if we let that happen, sea levels will rise by as much as six metres. Whole coastal regions will be lost, millions of lives. You think I'm just going to sit by and let that happen?"

You shook your head and smiled. "They're going to melt. The question is: what if we let them melt where a gazillion gallons of freshwater will do some good?"

• • •

The Chinook passes over Nouamghar and follows the conveyor belt. On either side, the scorched sands of the Western Sahara stretch to the shimmery horizon. From up here, the conveyor looks like a foot-wide black strip loaded with crushed ice. But I know its actual width, and my mind locks up trying to calculate how much water is travelling inland.

We're already raising the water table, Rowan. It took the fortune I amassed with sustainable energy, and draws every gigawatt of solar power from the Algerian farm, but it's happening.

Sixty miles inland, Melting Station A feeds the Benichab irrigation hub. From the helicopter, I look down upon the slowly expanding circle around the hub, the green land, wadis that used to be dry most of the year now supporting dates and coconuts and meadows.

You should have seen this.

ABOUT THE AUTHOR

Floris M. Kleijne is the author of over two dozen short stories in *Daily Science Fiction*, *Galaxy's Edge*, *Factor Four*, and numerous other publications. He lives in a 200-year-old house in the Dutch river district, but does most of his writing on trains. Floris was the first Dutchman to win the prestigious *Writers of the Future* contest, as well as the first Dutchman to qualify for active membership of the SFWA. He blogs about writing , Real Life™, and atrocious customer service on www.floriskleijne.com, where you can also read more of his stories.

BURIED PHOENIX. AND LEAVES

Y. M. Pang

I am the renewing flame, and you are the one I must burn.

I was taught this from the beginning, when my fire was only a spark, a bean-sized flicker on the end of a match. Father folded me in his arms and said, "Daughter, someday you will save the world."

Save the world. Burn the world. Cut out the rot from the world with my love's ashes as the dagger. All the same thing.

Love. Do I have the right to call you that?

When the day comes, when the moons kiss and the stars spin and the skies crackle like-lightning but not-lightning, I'll close my hands around your throat and shake you until your sixty thousand quadrillion leaves scatter onto paved roads, onto twisting skyscrapers and satellite dishes yawning at the sky like giant hollowed clams. Your leaves will rain onto forests piling with refuse, onto thinning ice where the last northern bear scrabbles, claws digging into seawater, fur streaked silver in the midnight sun.

Then I'll fly over the world on phoenix wings that block the sky while despoilers bury their faces in their hands, shielding their eyes from my searing light. I'll breathe my flame upon the world, onto the scattered leaves that are all that remain of you. I will burn every despoiler and all they've built, and the world will begin anew.

I knew this from the beginning. Still I couldn't help reaching out to you.

I met you by the river bisecting the starflower forest. Your hair was a weave of leaves strung down your back, the maples' sharp pen-nib tips just starting to turn red. Green vines crawled over your breasts like serpents. Your eyes, when you looked at me, held recognition. But you did not recoil. You did not ask what I—the renewing phoenix, the saviour, the end of the world—was doing in the sanctuary of the one I'd someday burn.

Instead, you said, "I'm so glad to meet you."

I could have filled in the unsaid part. "I'm so glad to meet you before the end." Or, "I'm so glad to meet you now, instead of when you're burning my scattered pieces."

River water sprayed across my arms, swift-moving and cold, but even it smelled of copper and arsenic, like some millennia-old beast had died there and still bled beneath the currents. "I shouldn't be here," I said. You only moved closer. "You should be afraid of me," I said, but you only smiled and said, "Who would fear the saviour of the world?"

I came back, day after day, though I should not.

I spoke to you, though I should not. I whispered, worried that a strong puff of my breath would set you alight.

One evening I reached for you. We touched. Just our fingertips, no more. You didn't burn and hope smouldered in my heart, though I knew we could not draw any closer.

I want … not to burn you. Not to stay like this forever either. But something in between. I want to embrace you but not consume you, or maybe consume you without erasing you, or maybe I don't know what I want at all and Father really should've kept a better watch on me.

The promised day creeps closer. Despoilers should be marking down the date on their dead trees, except they plod on unaware. I feel sorry for them. But most of all I feel sorry for you. The flame always falls for her fuel. But once in love, does the flame still want to burn—

To kill—?

Father is combing my hair, and the brush goes up in flames.

I face you, the night before the promised day, my

choice made. "Let's not do this," I say.

Your eyes widen and they are clear as lost rivers, dark as the night skies had been before light devoured them. "We must," you say.

I sweep a hand to encompass the skinny, twisting buildings that claw for the heavens like diseased mountains, to encompass the canals and ships and the hum of an underground generator that seems as entrenched as the song of the world. "I want to give them a chance," I say. I mean, "I want you to live."

Your lip trembles. Your hand brushes my cheek, though I'm so near awakening that your skin peels off and drifts away like slips of translucent plastic.

"Can they?" you say. "Can they fix what they've caused?"

"We have to trust them," I say.

I think, "I don't want you to die because of them."

It takes you an eternity to nod. I know what this means to you. Like me, you've been preparing for this moment your whole life. Like me, you know once the day passes we will not have another chance. It is the one day when your leaves reach their full growth, when my fire blazes at its very brightest, bright enough to burn-consume-save-destroy the world.

I am not prepared for what you do next.

You throw yourself against me, entwining your arms around mine like we are braided bamboo, laying your head on my shoulder so that my flesh brands your cheek autumn red. Your hair spills down my breastbone and begins to crisp away. "Burn me now," you say. "Burn me now so we'll both be gone. Burn me now so we can finally be …" Your breath hitches; you cannot bring yourself to finish that sentence.

I'm paralyzed. It's what I've always wanted, you so close to me, but in panic I can barely process what it feels like. Then instinct takes over: not to savour this, but to protect you.

"No!" I shove you away. My hands leave burning prints over your collarbones. "I want you to live."

Your tears water the dead leaves of your hair, the ruined skin of your torso. In places your skin has burned away completely, exposing streaks of yellow fat. I ache with want for you and pain at what I've done.

"Your scars will heal," I say. "The world will survive. You will find someone who loves you."

I don't know what I'm saying. I don't believe what I'm saying. I just know I am fire and you are leaves and I can save neither love nor world without destroying them first. And it's only a matter of time before Father realizes the promised day has come and gone without me carrying out my task.

So I flee. I fly to the sea and coalesce into myself, fold upon fold, like a many-layered origami flower or the collapsing pillars of a charred building. I throw myself into salt water, where I taste the sirens' tears and the filth of despoiler waste. I burrow into the sand of the ocean floor. I am barnacle, I am crab, I am a scuttling creature with needles for legs scratching at the armour of the world. I tunnel through the crust and sink to where heated rock melts. Then I fall deeper, into liquid metal.

There I swim, ever burning and ever burned. Metal fills my ears and mouth, and I shape it into pearls on my tongue. I dream of your autumn-kissed leaves and the trust in your eyes, and I watch you as you watch the world. My voice weaves a harmony beneath the world's song and the hum of the generator. I sing of the truth we share, of a choice made for the wrong reasons and the best reasons: the world wasn't saved by mercy, but by love.

ABOUT THE AUTHOR

Y. M. Pang spent her childhood pacing around her grandfather's bedroom, telling him stories of magic, swords, and bears. Her fiction has appeared in *The Magazine of Fantasy & Science Fiction*, *Strange Horizons*, and *Escape Pod*, among other venues. She lives in Canada, where she dabbles in photography and often contemplates the merits of hermitism. Despite this, you can find her online at www.ympang.com and on Twitter as @YMPangWriter.

ADVICE FOR GIRLS
WHO WORRY ABOUT
CLIMATE CHANGE

Alice Towey

You must hold the earth gently
like you hold this monarch,
newly emerged from its chrysalis,
as it pauses on your fingertips to flex its wings.

See how it decides all at once—
sweeping open its delicate silks
of black and orange, how it lifts off
and careens through the air.

Not much luck for butterflies. Each year
the news is worse: heat waves
rippling forests into char, brutal highways,
and fields stripped bare of grass and thistle.

One could so easily give up. Stop bringing
the caterpillars indoors to safety. Stop
watering the milkweed in your backyard
with shower remnants from a plastic bucket.

You must find new ways to love,
in contradiction: love the flower
like you discovered it, love the monarch
like you'll be the last person to see one alive.

Trust in a future where butterflies
still flicker through a garden
to alight on each bright summer blossom,
if you can just keep this generation

alive.

ABOUT THE AUTHOR

Alice Towey is a writer of speculative fiction and poetry
based out of Northern California. A graduate of the Viable
Paradise workshop, her short fiction will be included in the
forthcoming anthology, *A Flash of Silver Green: Stories of the
Nature of Cities*. When she isn't writing, Towey works as a civil
engineer specializing in water resource management.

ABOUT THE EDITOR

Katrina Archer is the author of dark fantasy *The Tree of Souls* and YA fantasy *Untalented*, a *Library Journal* Indie Ebook Award Honorable Mention. A former software engineer, she lives on her sailboat in Vancouver, BC, Canada. Katrina has worked in aerospace, video games, and film, and is a freelance copy editor and publisher of climate change site *Little Blue Marble*. She can operate almost any vehicle that can't fly, doesn't believe in life without books or chocolate, and was once owned by a cat more famous in Germany than she is. Connect with her online at www.katrinaarcher.com.

READ MORE

For more great fiction and features about
our changing climate, join us at

LittleBlueMarble.ca

Also available from *Little Blue Marble:*

*Little Blue Marble 2017: Stories of Our
Changing Climate*

*Little Blue Marble 2018: More Stories of Our
Changing Climate*